Agnes Bailey Ormsbee

The house comfortable by Agnes Bailey Ormsbee

Agnes Bailey Ormsbee

The house comfortable by Agnes Bailey Ormsbee

ISBN/EAN: 9783743329928

Manufactured in Europe, USA, Canada, Australia, Japa

Cover: Foto ©Andreas Hilbeck / pixelio.de

Manufactured and distributed by brebook publishing software
(www.brebook.com)

Agnes Bailey Ormsbee

The house comfortable by Agnes Bailey Ormsbee

THE HOUSE COMFORTABLE

BY

AGNES BAILEY ORMSBEE

NEW YORK

HARPER & BROTHERS, FRANKLIN SQUARE

1892

TO

H. S. B.

THE WISE MOTHER WHO TAUGHT ME ALL
HOMELY WAYS AND SO MADE THIS
LITTLE BOOK POSSIBLE

CONTENTS.

CHAP.		PAGE
I.	"EVERY WISE WOMAN BUILDETH HER HOUSE".	I
II.	THE USE OF SMALL MEANS.	8
III.	UNDERLYING ALL	17
IV.	"THE VERY PULSE OF THE MACHINE".	27
V.	FURNISHING THE DINING-ROOM	40
VI.	TABLE APPOINTMENTS	50
VII.	SILVER AND GLASS	62
VIII.	UNDERFOOT	74
IX.	CARE OF ·FLOORS AND FURNITURE	85
X.	FURNISHING SLEEPING-ROOMS	95
XI.	SHEETS, BLANKETS, AND TOWELS.	106
XII.	CURTAINS, SCREENS, DRAPERIES, AND RUGS.	117
XIII.	THE FAMILY HEARTH-STONE	126
XIV.	THE KING'S DOMAIN	136
XV.	"SHE MAKETH HERSELF COVERINGS".	146
XVI.	PICTURES FOR THE HOME	155

CHAP.   PAGE

XVII. THE POWER OF COLOR 164

XVIII. WITH PIPE AND SLIPPERS 173

XIX. HALLS AND WALLS 181

XX. THE PARLOR 191

XXI. LIBRARY AND MUSIC-ROOM 200

XXII. TREASURE-CHAMBERS 209

XXIII. A CATCH-ALL CHAPTER 217

XXIV. OUT IN THE BACK YARD 226

THE HOUSE COMFORTABLE.

I.

"EVERY WISE WOMAN BUILDETH HER HOUSE."

To achieve the House Comfortable it is necessary to start with sound principles, and to keep constantly in mind the ends for which a home is established. A home should yield rest, refreshment, and inspiration to the members of the family; should be the place in which each member gathers renewed courage. It follows, then, that those parts of the house which most affect the daily health and happiness of the household should be equipped first and most thoroughly, and that those rooms which are shared with the outside world should not be beautified at the expense of more important portions.

A well-furnished and well-managed kitchen, which shall daily send forth three savory meals, and from which the spirit of strife shall not arise, filling the whole house like a miasma, is of more moment in the House Comfortable than a drawing-room that shall be the envy of every woman who sees it. Sleeping-rooms supplied with the best springs, mattresses, and blankets, and filled with an atmosphere that is fresh but not raw, and mild without stuffiness, are to be preferred before the costliest carved cabinet from Holland, filled with treasures from Vienna.

It is not that a beautiful drawing-room is not a desirable thing. It is as goodly and attractive in the House Comfortable as elsewhere. It does contribute more than a little to the comfort of the woman who has planned it, and of the husband whose house and whose wife are admired because of its beauty. The point is that it is not the first thing, or the second thing, perhaps not even the third thing; that if need be the House

Comfortable can flourish without it, and that if the money at hand is limited, the drawing-room should be considered last, and that in any case it should not usurp an undue proportion of thought and attention.

In furnishing a home of seven or eight rooms, unless a lavish use of money is possible, the money may well be divided into three equal parts, to be distributed among the three floors of a city house—one-third for the basement, of kitchen and dining-room, one-third for the parlor floor, and one-third for the sleeping-rooms. In a country house the arrangement of the rooms is different, but the proportion of money for the three classes of rooms should be substantially the same. Where the supply of money is practically unlimited, there will naturally be a larger number of rooms to furnish, and the distribution of the increased money is largely a matter of taste. But in such a case, if the House Comfortable is desired rather than the House Artistic or the Castle Display, it will be the part of wisdom to make liberal appropriations for the kitchen, and, above all, for the dining-room, where a lavish use of artistically beautiful furnishings, of fine linens and dainty china, is more conducive to comfort than in any other part of the house. It is also wise to provide well for the sitting-rooms, the smoking-room, the nursery, the sewing and sleeping rooms, rather than to reserve the bulk of the expenditure for the drawing-rooms, and leave the rest of the house to be filled up by chance. The latter course is too often followed by those who have much money as well as by those with little. As to that large class of people who must furnish, if they furnish at all, on a much smaller scale, their case is by no means hopeless, but it requires more careful and detailed consideration than can be given in a general introductory chapter.

A prime consideration in making the House Comfortable is what things to buy, and of what quality they shall be. A dividing line can be drawn through the whole household belongings, from cellar to attic. This line runs between things for use and things for decoration. Some articles, of course, serve both uses, but in each instance it is easy to decide for which quality the particular object is bought.

For the two classes of furnishings, two distinct rules hold good. In buying things for use "the best is none too good"—best in this connection meaning, of course, most durable or best adapted for use. There are woods and other materials which are expensive because they are scarce or fashionable, there are fabrics and articles of furniture which are costly because they are of a novel weave or design, which are no better for the House Comfortable than less costly but equally durable and useful substitutes. A mahogany table is no better than one of oak, except as it gratifies one's pride; but a weak-legged or tottlish table, a rickety or penitentially straight-backed chair, or a right-angled and lignumvitæ-stuffed sofa is a torment, no matter how picturesque or "stylish" its form.

In giving a home-like air by means of decorative touches present effect is desired rather than durability. Now warmth and richness of tone depend more upon other elements than upon the cost of the materials with which they are produced. Even striking artistic beauty can be obtained at trifling cost if one but have the artistic eye. The skilful and delicate use of color is more potent in producing warmth, richness, cosiness, in a room than the wealth of an Astor would be, applied without the oversight of trained skill. We have all seen rooms which had "nothing in them," from the auctioneer's point of view, yet in which the spirit of domestic comfort seemed to have her perpetual abode.

Another reason for the sparing use of money in decorations is that "old things pass away" with surprising quickness in house furnishings. This is an era of rapid artistic development as applied to household belongings, and we have by no means reached the limits of growth. The beautiful thing of to-day is succeeded by the more beautiful thing of next week, and the enjoyment of the average mortal in his possessions is much lessened when they have gone hopelessly and irredeemably out of fashion. An easy and substantial chair or a well-built table of handsome wood, providing it be not ugly in shape, is still a substantial and respectable piece of furniture after its particular vogue has departed, and it will adapt itself surprisingly well to a new scheme of decoration and color. But a china plaque, unless it be a remarkable work of art, is not a comfort in an era when every one uses brass sconces, nor will heavy, stolid plush draperies be a joy when the reign of lighter, more graceful hangings shall have come in.

To summarize, in the House Comfortable use comes before display, health before fashion, and adaptability to present and future circumstances is considered in the buying of all its belongings. With these ideas in mind, and with a determination to adapt the house to the particular needs of the family which will dwell in it, one cannot go far astray.

II.

THE USE OF SMALL MEANS.

IT is not so astonishing as it would seem at first that many really home-loving young married couples delay the making of the home, and temporize with the perplexing problem by boarding for a while. It is useless to say that none should marry until there are means at hand to provide a home. Circumstances, inexperience, and a heedless happy - go - lucky trust in the future, bring about fully as many marriages as do prudence, thrift, or happily filled purses. The establishing of a home is made an anxious, troublesome matter, because it does cost a good deal of money, and because few are willing to be honest and make no more display than they can afford, regardless of the comments of acquaintances.

A house of moderate size, say, from six to

eight rooms, furnished throughout, without any effort at display or decorative attempts beyond the tasteful choosing of plain but durable furniture, will cost upwards of eight hundred dollars. There is an incalculable number of small necessities, from the rolling-pin in the pantry to the water-pitcher in the chamber, which cost very little when reckoned singly, but whose united demand on the purse is not small. With the large items of stove and table, chairs and beds, mattresses and lamps, the total quickly grows. Although this complete furnishing is beyond the reach of many, homes can *begin* with a smaller amount. And fortunately most newly-married couples do not have to buy everything. Wedding presents and the bride's outfit go a long way towards reducing the expense, and supplying those pretty things which add so greatly to the cosey look of a home.

To make this beginning a happy and a prosperous one, it is absolutely necessary that there should be a perfect understanding and unity of purpose between the husband and the wife. They should know exactly how they intend to spend the money at their command, and what purchases and what sacrifices will satisfy their mutual ideas of the home they are beginning. Blame for the tendency to display and showiness in a house is usually laid on the wife's shoulders. This is not just. In fully half the cases the husband's pride is as much the cause as the wife's vanity.

The young man, good and kindly without doubt, is earning twelve hundred dollars. He has found that sum ample for his needs, has been particular that his coat, his hat, his scarf, were all as the season's fashions prescribed. He has dressed nearly as well as his friend who has twice his income. When it comes to making a home, the difference between the two incomes is felt at once. His pride steps in. He cannot bear that his little parlor shall be a whit less fine than his friend's. There must be ornaments and drapery and fine furniture which will still keep up the illusion as to income that his faultless clothing did in his single days. The wife, forty times out of fifty, wishes to please her husband, and, as a result, a miserable series of purchases is made, while the real needs of the home are neglected. This constant strain to cheat the public by an appearance of greater prosperity than exists is far more disastrous to family comfort than honestly but tacitly acknowledging the limitations of the purse.

When false pride has been conquered and a mutual agreement has been reached, the use of small means can begin successfully. The actual needs should be the first to receive attention. These consist largely in furniture—the table to eat on, the chairs to sit on, the beds to sleep in. Let each article be thoroughly good of its kind. Let no piece of furniture be bought that is not solid and of honest strength and durability. The parlor table may be plain, but let it be so genuine that when prosperous days come, and it is relegated to the sitting-room, nursery, or sewing-room to give place to its more elegant successor, it may yet be useful and substantial. As nearly as possible buy every bit of furniture with the idea that it is to last your lifetime, and try to choose such pieces as will be comfortable and satisfactory twenty years hence. Scratches and mars that use always brings can be "dressed out" of good wood, but ill-shaped pieces will ever be an annoyance; and furniture which refuses to stay together, over which screws and joints have no control, never ceases to be a trouble, and sooner or later represents so much money almost thrown away, even though the veneer and carving in its first estate were most attractive.

Home-made furniture is rarely successful and more rarely economical. Occasionally a husband or wife has a gift at carpentry, and can do wonders. If the young husband can build furniture so well that he would not hesitate to offer to sell it, with a fair likelihood of getting a purchaser, let him build all he can for his home. It will be good, and of as much comfort to the household as the dainty needle-work his wife may have the skill to fashion. But let the ordinary wielder of the hammer, saw, and plane beware. The materials used will usually cost half enough to buy the finished article at a reliable shop. After the furniture is done, and money, time, and strength have been devoted to it, what is the usual result? A "toggled-up" article that is rarely comfortable, generally cumbersome, and will come to pieces within a year. A chair made out of a barrel is always a barrel, even though covered with raw silk and adorned with velours squares. Far better an honest cane-seated rocker than such a hypocritical, vulgar makeshift.

It is perhaps excusable and defensible to supply the most pressing needs of furnishing, which sometimes accumulate with discouraging frequency, by paying for them in instalments, but it is an unfortunate recourse. Not alone does the purchaser pay higher prices, but he rarely gets as good an article. The buyer on credit cannot trade at the best advantage. He often buys what he does not like or want, because he must trade where he can and not where his choice leads him. Besides, this mortgaging future earnings brings a wretchedly anxious state of mind, especially to the young man on a small salary or the small tradesman. This anxiety robs him of much satisfaction in the purchase, and he is fortunate indeed if sickness or some sudden emergency does not make it impossible to meet his stated payment.

Buy as few necessities as possible without paying for them, and never, never buy anything not absolutely necessary without the money in your hand to pay for it. Small means are trying to the patience and pin-pricking to the tastes and longings, but not half so harassing as debts. There is nothing decorative about unpaid bills. There is comfort where one can say "a poor thing, but *mine own*." Contentment, happiness, and thrift form a joyous trio in such a home though in its most humble beginning.

In cities living in flats gives home-makers as good a chance to begin in a small way as perhaps anywhere in the world. The rooms are proverbially small, but this is an advantage for the time being. Few pieces of furniture will be needed for any room, and these can be so chosen as to fit in harmoniously when larger quarters demand additions to the store. Apartment-houses are furnished with window-shades and inside blinds, so there need be no outlay in that direction. The kitchen has its range and stationary tubs already built in. The floors are well laid and sometimes already stained, so that carpets are not required. Indeed, the present fashion or sanitary crusade against carpets is one of the greatest helps to scantily filled purses. Household gods can be cosily set up without this heavy outlay, while one rug after another can gradually be brought to soften and ornament the neatly stained floors.

If one's lot is cast in the country and not in a house of recent building, the carpet question looms up threateningly, because the floors are too poor and uneven for painting or staining. Matting is the least expensive —at first cost—of any floor-covering in such a case, and the home-maker will have to content herself with the thoughts of the cheaper daily expenses, while her sister in the city flat groans over the cost of living from hand to mouth which the small apartment compels.

A pleasant way of obtaining the little luxuries, the oft-promised additional furniture, the dainty drapery and pretty trifles which are so much treasured by every one, is to mark each birthday, Christmas, or domestic anniversary by some addition to home comfort or ornament instead of remembrances for purely personal use. Almost any housewife would delight in such a plan and would take genuine pleasure in each gift. While her better half might not indulge in as much mild ecstasy as she, his secret pride would be gratified to see furnishings accumulating, and ornaments gradually and tastefully veiling the hard outlines of his home.

Full directions for beginning a little home and prices of furniture cannot be compressed into one chapter, but the necessities of such furnishing will be considered in detail later.

III.

UNDERLYING ALL.

WHEN the house-keeper has bought, built, or hired her house, after due consideration of the family needs and tastes, and after careful examination of the locality and construction of the chosen home, her earliest attention should be directed to the cellar, as that part of the home which is most often neglected, and where order and convenience combined add no small amount to the comfort and healthfulness of all parts of the house.

The arrangement of the cellar takes time and attention rather than any great outlay of money. The windows should first be seen to. A stuffy, unventilated cellar, full of dead air, is an abomination. The windows should be so hung that they can be removed from the inside, and during all but

2

the extreme winter months should be taken out, and even then in mild days they should be opened in the middle of the day. The outside of the windows should be protected by galvanized wire window-netting, costing two and a half cents the square foot. A heavier, coarser-meshed quality can be used instead, if great strength is desired. This quality cost six cents the square foot. The hatchways of city houses are troublesome in cold weather. Both the rear and front hatchways admit a great deal of wind during the winter, in spite of the wooden covers that are fitted to them, and make the kitchen and dining-room floors draughty and cold. This can be remedied by covering the iron grating over each hatchway with several folds of old carpeting or furniture sacking, and then fitting the cover down tightly. The hatchway on the sunny side of the house must be frequently opened for air. The cellar ceiling and walls should be thoroughly whitewashed, two heavy coats being enough.

All city cellars, and many in the country towns and villages, are cemented, which un-

der most conditions is the safest and cleanest flooring. But in the country, where the
ground is not poisoned from leakages of
sewers or the foul gases of cesspools, and
where, yet further, the ground is dry and
sandy, a cellar bottom of well-beaten earth
is not unwholesome, and has a mysterious
capacity for keeping fruits and vegetables
beyond that of cemented cellars. Such a
cellar should have boards for walks to bins,
barrels, and cupboard, to keep the house
mother from fretting over the dirt "tracked
up."   If these boards are occasionally turned over when swept, there will be no trouble
from dampness or "saw bugs."   Raising
them up slightly from the ground by inch
cleats nailed to the under-side of the boards
is another and better method.

In a cellar where there is a furnace, it is
a great help to household management to
have a portion of the cellar divided from the
furnace portion by a tight board partition,
with a padlocked door opening into it. The
boards used may be rough and cheap, costing two cents a foot ; but the partition must
be tight, so as not to admit the warm air

from the furnace.   Under ordinary circumstances the expense need not be over ten
dollars, and in many cases even less.

In this cold cellar the vegetables and apples, butter and preserves, may be kept, and
even in the city the uncomfortable habit of
living from hand to mouth might be changed
to a great degree.   Here the time-honored
vinegar barrel or keg may have its place,
giving out its supply of "pure cider" vinegar whenever needed.   Near by should be
the swinging shelf and cupboard, and the
old-time feeling of plenty and comfort, which
the memory of the well-filled cellars of country homes always brings, would return to
the household.

It is convenient and desirable in a permanent home to have bins built for the various
vegetables and fruits.   But in homes that
are ours only by virtue of a lease, barrels or
boxes answer the purpose, and at the same
time are kept ready for use in the next family flight.   The cover of each box should be
carefully saved, the long nails having been
drawn out and placed behind the box, where
they can easily be found.   Boxes are better

than barrels for this use, because they are more shallow and the vegetables can be spread over a wider surface, enabling decaying or poor specimens to be more easily seen and removed. Boxes, barrels, firkins, or stone jars ought never to be set directly on the cellar bottom. They should be put on bricks, stones, or small pieces of board : a brick at each corner being enough to balance any large box. This makes it easier to move in cleaning or to handle these boxes, and the little air passage beneath prevents any serious gathering of dampness or decaying of the wood.

Every cellar should have one swinging shelf, stoutly held by supports at the four corners, nailed to the floor joists above. It can be made a double or single shelf, three feet wide and eight feet long, but must be strongly fastened, lest the house-keeper some day hear an ominous crash, later to find her precious jars of fruit, her pies and cookies, all hopelessly mingled on the cellar bottom and full of broken glass.

A cupboard which can stand securely on the cellar floor, and which is closed by a door, is better for the canned or preserved fruit, the jellies, jams, and bottled pickles; for such are like evil men, preferring darkness rather than light.   Pickles, both sweet and sour, in any quantity, can more safely and easily be kept in small stone crocks, and can be set in orderly rows about the cellar bottom.   The wood, usually pine, for the cupboard and swinging shelf will not cost a great deal, the principal expense being the day's work of the carpenter.   Occasionally the housewife's husband is that rare being "a handy man," and can construct these conveniences himself, which is, of course, all the better for the family purse.

A wire cupboard is wellnigh indispensable.   It is built exactly like a double swinging shelf.   There should be double frame doors on one side, hung to open outward, fastening with a button.   Then the back and the doors should be covered with galvanized wire fly netting.   This netting will not rust, and such a cupboard will last a lifetime.   Five to six feet is a good length for this cupboard, and one foot and a half a good width.   The cost should not exceed five dollars, and can be lessened if the housewife will buy the netting and tack it on herself. Even common cotton mosquito bar will do, but it will have to be renewed yearly. Here, in summer weather, the cold roasts or uncooked meats can stand without harm. Here the bread, which would mould in the kitchen pantry, will keep sweet and moist, and the milk and vegetables, which the ice-chest is often too crowded to hold, will keep fresh and crisp in the cool, changing, flyless air.

A small box of sand is excellent to keep celery in, and should take its place beside the other boxes. The sand should be renewed yearly, and every decaying or vagrant stalk should be carefully picked out. A small stone crock or butter firkin filled with brine ("strong enough to float an egg," was our grandmother's safe rule) should be ready, into which the small pieces of salt pork from the butcher's should always be dropped, and weighed down with a clean stone or earthen plate.

The cellar in city houses has often to serve not alone in its proper capacity, but

also as wood-shed and attic. Nothing should
be kept in the cold cellar but food. A bin
to hold the coal should be strongly built in
the furnace part of the cellar, and near the
hatchway or coal-hole, that the coal may be
thrown directly into it. A small section of
the walls of the bin should be made of movable boards in order to get at the coal. A
scoop shovel for shovelling the coal should
be bought, and will cost sixty-five cents. A
small iron shovel is equally necessary for
filling the scuttles, and will cost forty cents.
A couple of big nails driven into the bin
posts, on which to hang these shovels, will
save the annoyance so often endured when
a carelessly dropped shovel has been forgotten and buried by the coming of the next
load of coal.

The same disposition should be made of
the axe or hatchet for splitting wood and
kindlings. Two nails or a strap of leather
fastened to a post will keep a sixty-five-cent
hatchet always at hand, and preserve at the
same time its temper and that of its user.
A thick piece of floor joist should always
be provided to chop kindlings on, that the

cement floor may not be ruined. Furnace ashes should never be emptied in the cellar, but put in barrels or boxes outside the house, as is done with the ashes from the stoves.

When the cellar must be used for storage purposes, only things of actual value and possible usefulness should be kept. Anything that is worn out or has been succeeded by an article of greater helpfulness should be thrown or given away. If an article is broken, but can be mended and reused, let the mending be done before it is stored away. The cellar is a poor attic at best; but when it must be used, let every article be well tied up in stout wrapping-paper, furniture sacking, or bits of old carpet. Then hang everything possible, from the unused baby-carriage to a tin pail, from the beams of the ceiling, with nails, screws, and strong cords. Discretion should be used not to hang articles in the pathway to the furnace, the bins, or the cold cellar. When this hanging has been well done, the comfort of sweeping and examining the cellar without having to handle and move things not in actual use will be speedily felt. When stationary tubs are not built in the kitchen the movable tubs have to be kept carefully that they do not dry up and fall to pieces, and should be turned bottom up on the cellar floor away from the furnace. These tubs and their companion scrubbing-pails might be put in the cold cellar. The safest light to carry to the cellar where there is no gas-jet is the old-fashioned sperm candle in a broad-bottomed tin candlestick.

IV.

"THE VERY PULSE OF THE MACHINE."

THE novice is apt to think that the needs of the kitchen are trifling, and that purchases for it can be placed, like itself, quite in the rear of all else.   But the truth is that the kitchen table is even more necessary than a drawing-room table, and that kitchen furnishings are really formidable rivals in expense to those in "the front room."

All kitchen utensils and furniture should be carefully bought, for they are the tools by which the health of the household is wrought.   Health-giving food and clean apparel come from within the kitchen walls, and whatever cripples its efforts to provide these is lamentable, and should have no place in the House Comfortable.   Scanty, poor utensils affect the variety, quality, and palatableness of food, and unnecessarily wear out the worker's strength and temper. This needless waste of strength, even in a servant, is poor economy, and in the kitchen the builder of a home should relax her desire to save, and freely and cheerfully provide all that her practical sense of family comfort shows to be needed.

The kitchen stove or range is the first thing to be bought. This is a large expenditure, but not to be avoided, unless the home-maker lives in a large city. There the range is built into the house, and into the better apartments. Such ranges are set into the chimney, hence the name " brick-set," and they cost from $18 to $75, according to size and quality. The price includes the pipes and all the connections with the tall cylindrical copper hot-water boiler that stands in the chimney-corner. The best ranges come from Troy, though Philadelphia ranges are cheaper. But those ranges in which the hot-water boiler is set above the range, in place of the oven, and the oven itself placed below the fire-box, are poor ones, and do not give good service. They are used by builders in cities, as they lessen the plumber's bill, which the copper boiler and its pipes help to swell.

Next to the "brick-set" is the "portable" range, looking like the cooking-stove of twenty years ago, but fitted with all the modern appliances for saving both heat and fuel. These ranges are supplied with two grates, so that either coal or wood may be burned. All portable ranges can have the pipes, called "water front," of a boiler connected with them, and the larger ranges have the less modern reservoir attached to them to use where the water supply does not have sufficient force to fill a boiler. These ranges cost from $6 to $50, and the cost of the hot-water connection is included in the higher prices. The $6 range is a tiny affair for light house-keeping, with two griddle-holes and a wee oven, but does good work in miniature. Thirty dollars will buy a range of full size, and capable of doing all required for a large family. The high-priced ranges are more ornamental in casting, elaborately trimmed with nickel, but have no actual improvements beyond those in ranges of modest price.

The next purchases are those which may

be called kitchen furniture. One large table is needed; and a small one, three feet long and on casters, is useful for rolling about the room to save steps. These, two chairs, an alarm-clock, a lamp, a large pail, preferably one of paper that will not shrink, and one or two good brooms will take $7, which is a small outlay. If the small table is covered with zinc, it will be serviceable to set hot dishes on, and will cost $2 extra. Ten dollars will buy a marble-topped table mounted on pine, which is useful for pastry-making, especially in summer.

An excellent list of cooking utensils is given by Mrs. Christine Terhune Herrick in *House-keeping Made Easy*, which first appeared serially in HARPER'S BAZAR. This tabulation is quoted here as a guide in buying kitchen and pantry utensils:

THE MUST-HAVES.

One large dishpan for kitchen.	One dozen patty-pans, for muffins and small cakes.
One divided dishpan for dining-room.	Two small round cake-tins.
One large dripping-pan.	Four jelly-cake-tins.
One small dripping-pan.	Cake-cutters.
Three breadpans.	One dozen muffin-rings.
One biscuit-pan.	One chopping-bowl.
One round fluted cake-tin.	One bread-bowl.
	One chopping-knife.

One one-quart tin saucepan.
One two-quart tin saucepan.
One two-quart saucepan, agate-ware or porcelain-lined.
One one-quart saucepan, agate-ware or porcelain-lined.
One frying-pan.
One soup-kettle, agate-ware or porcelain-lined.
One four-quart tin pail.
One two-quart tin pail.
One one-quart tin pail.
One graduated quart measure.
One half-pint tin cup.
One tin dipper.
One cake-turner.
One corkscrew.
One pastry-jagger.
One wash-basin.
One towel-roller.
A six-quart seamless milk-pan.
A four-quart seamless milk-pan.
Two jelly moulds.
One plain pudding mould.
One two-quart pitcher.
One four-quart pitcher.
Four yellow mixing bowls, assorted sizes.
Two small yellow bowls.
One split spoon.
Two wooden spoons.
Two iron spoons.
Six kitchen knives.
Six kitchen forks.
Six teaspoons.
Three table-spoons.
One bread-knife.
One meat-knife.
One small knife for peeling potatoes, cutting the meat from bones, etc.
One larding-needle.
One soup-strainer.

One hair-wire gravy-strainer.
One colander.
One wire dishcloth.
One can-opener.
One apple-corer.
One large funnel.
One small funnel.
One bread-box.
One cake-box.
One potato beetle.
One meat broiler.
One fish broiler.
One toaster.
One vegetable grater.
One nutmeg grater.
Dredging boxes for salt, pepper, and flour.
Three pie-plates.
One lemon-squeezer.
One floor mop.
One dish mop.
One bread-board.
One small meat-board.
One rolling-pin.
Two sugar buckets.
One meal bucket.
One spice-box.
Scrubbing-brushes.
One garbage-pail of galvanized [iron.
One flour-barrel cover.
Knife and fork box.
One double boiler.
One teakettle.
One teapot.
One coffee-pot.
One Dover egg-beater.
Six kitchen plates.
Six kitchen cups and saucers.
Two large stone-ware platters.
One perforated skimmer.
One griddle.
Set of scales.
Two stone crocks.

Not one of the utensils of this list is unnec-
essary or extravagant in quality for the comfortable, strength-conserving doing of domestic cookery, and yet they give a total of $32
—the actual cost determined by careful pric-
ing of each article. The itemized list stands :
tins, $10; wooden-ware, $5 ; iron-ware, including household scales, $6; earthen-ware,
$4; agate-ware kettles, $3 ; cutlery, $3 ; ja-
panned boxes for bread, cake, and spices, $1.

There is never any economy in buying
even kitchen knives of anything but wrought
steel. Other knives will not take a good
edge, or stay sharp more than overnight.
Regular cooks' knives, such as are used by
professional *chefs*, would be a great help to
the ordinary housewife. Such small knives
cost $1.25, and larger ones more than that.
Agate-ware would be better than so much
tin-ware. It is light, durable, and easily
cleaned, but costs about twice as much.
But with ordinary usage it will last a long
time, not rusting or cracking, while food will
not burn as quickly in cooking.

The laundry work usually done at home
demands quite an array of articles. The

boiler, of good tin and with copper bottom and cover, costs $1.25. The clothes-horse, ironing and shirt boards, flat-irons, rub-boards, each moderate in its cost, help swell the list, until, when the clothes-line, pins, and basket are bought, $7 are spent, and yet there is no wringer. As with sewing-machines, so with wringers. There are several makes equally good and serviceable and almost alike, so it is hard to decide between them. Those that have the least complicated machinery require less careful handling and get out of order less often. The iron frame has the advantage of strength, while the wooden one is lighter. Four dollars buys a good one, and if its screws are kept from dampness, and rust is removed by kerosene, your chosen wringer will last for years. If stationary tubs are not in the house, portable ones must be bought, $2 buying two of medium size. This makes a total for laundry furnishings of $14.25.

A refrigerator or ice-chest is another "must have." An ice-chest is the cheapest, and a small one of grained wood, zinc-lined and with wire shelves, costs $3, each larger

3

size adding a dollar more to the cost. Such chests open only at the top, and all the shelves must be taken out to place the ice at the bottom. Then, the shelves replaced, the food is arranged on them. This inconvenience of having to place and replace the food—for it is the dish at the bottom that is sure to be wanted—is a great disadvantage, and partly offsets the ice-chest's valuable quality—economical ice consumption.

The cheapest refrigerator to be had is one which is zinc-lined, its walls packed with felt paper, and its shelves are of perforated zinc. This refrigerator has two openings, a double-lidded one at the top into the ice compartment; and the other, a single door in the front into the food-chamber. These two compartments are connected by two air-passages, and the waste-pipe has a siphon at its end to prevent the outer air from entering and melting the ice. A small size of this kind costs $6, keeps the food well, and does not need a large quantity of ice. Another style for $8 is almost identical, except that its shelves are made of galvanized iron, and are stronger than those of zinc.

The finest and most satisfactory refrigerator is zinc-lined, and packed with charcoal—the best non-conductor of heat for such uses. Its waste-pipe is double-siphoned, and has a movable elbow in the centre, so that the pipe can be easily cleaned. Its shelves are of galvanized iron, and its two divisions open by doors in front, one above the other. The divisions are connected by six passages, to make the air circulation as perfect as possible. This kind in medium size is $10.50. Each larger size is $3 more respectively. Another style of the same is made in hardwood, with some ornamentation, and is designed for flats and apartments where space must be closely utilized. These " flat " refrigerators are tall and narrow, but have all the economic and hygienic features of the ordinary ones, and, with finer wood-work, are an admissible part of dining-room furnishings whenever it is desirable. They cost respectively $13, $17, and $20, according to capacity.

The necessary kitchen furnishings having been discussed and their cost practically averaged, let us see how much money has been spent: Cooking utensils, $32; kitchen furniture, $7; laundry utensils, $13; refrigerator, $10—total, $62. If a range must be bought, it will add $30 more. Each home should have its individual and special likes and needs. These will be felt more or less in the kitchen purchases, causing some things to be bought which no list of needs can dictate. If the home-maker furnishes her kitchen, including range, for $100, she may rest satisfied that it is in reality a small sum, spent to the best advantage for her home's welfare.

Among the labor-saving and comfort-providing appliances for domestic use are the gas and kerosene stoves. These are boons to the housewife during warm weather, and are economical in every particular, saving food, fuel, and strength. The number of hot dishes for each meal is limited by the capacity of the stove; but this is rather an added gain. Too many hot dishes are neither palatable nor healthful.

In cities and towns where gas rates are as low as $1.50 a thousand feet a gas-stove is as cheap as an oil-stove, and is odorless,

cleaner, safer, and less trouble to manage.
The heat is intense but even, and all broil-
ing, frying, boiling, and steaming is rapidly
done. The gas - stove requires no special
utensils. Those used on any range are
equally well adapted for it, and it can be
placed wherever connection can be made
with any ordinary gas-burner.

A two-burner gas-stove has done for two
years the ironing of a family of five, two of
them being children, and all the meals and
cooking during three months, excepting a
range fire to heat the washing-water on Mon-
day, and sufficient fire on Wednesday and
Saturday to bake bread, cake, and the like.
The stove cost $4, and five feet of rubber
tubing to connect with the small kitchen burner cost 50 cents. Its use increased the gas
bill about $1 a month. Gas-stoves are made
with one, two, three, and four burners, and
the larger ones have ovens; but the average
price of a two-burner is $4, and this, as has
been said, can be made to do good service.

It is difficult to choose an oil-stove, each
kind having its good qualities, and all being
economical and manageable with care and

cleanliness. The tiny one-burner comes at less than a dollar, while two, three, and four burners increase in price and completeness of utensils, till we have one almost equal to a range. It now remains for some genius to invent an attachment to heat the hot-water boiler of the range, and then all house-wives will say good-bye to range, scuttle, and coal-bin from June to October. A two-burner oil-stove, with a fair supply of utensils, will cost about $5, and the amount of work done by it depends upon the "faculty" of its user.

An ice-cream freezer is an addition in providing delicacies for the table at small outlay, and is now in common use in many households. There are various makes in the market, several of those recently invented working very rapidly and easily. They hold from two quarts to twenty-four, the former size costing $1.70.

A steam-cooker is expensive at first, costing from $5 to $7, but is most economical and helpful, and lasts a lifetime.

One of the best cookers has a small division at the bottom for the water which makes the steam. Above it are several other divisions, separated from each other by perforated tin disks. The whole looks like an elongated tin pail, standing three feet high, and large enough to hold an entire dinner. The tight cover prevents the escape of any odor, and many kinds of meat, fish, and vegetables are superior in flavor from this mode of cooking. A whistle signals when the water needs replenishing, and by a tube the water is easily added. Such a cooker is equally adaptable to the range and oil or gas stoves, and is especially easy to can fruit by.

English porcelain covered jars, graduated in size, to hold supplies, are a great improvement in the pantry. Each jar is plainly labelled, and this prevents mistakes which haste and carelessness make in getting materials for cooking. The neat, tidy appearance of the pantry is also enhanced by the use of such jars. The small spice-jars are 20 cents, while the largest one, holding five pounds of flour, is $1.75. The same jars in blue and white porcelain cost from 60 cents to $2.50.

V.

FURNISHING THE DINING-ROOM.

THE house-keeper's first efforts in furnishing and arranging her dining-room, whether in a modest cottage or apartment-house or in the home of ample means, should be to make it a cheerful room. It is the gathering-place of the whole family, and much influence over these tri-daily unions is exerted by the outward aspect of the room itself. It is not enough that it be clean and dustless, in good order and freshly aired, but its pervading expression must be one of good cheer.

The walls and ceilings should be light in tone. Buff, terra-cotta, or pale yellow-green are among the best tints. Painted walls are the cleanest, for dust, traces of flies, and odors of food which cling to the wall are easily removed by washing, or brushing down and dusting with a damp cloth. It costs considerable to paint walls, as they need at least three coats, besides the first coat of "sizing" to keep the paint from sinking in. The decorative effect and the expense may be made still greater by painting the cornice in harmonious contrasting colors. If the ceiling is high, this border can be made wide; but if low, a band of one color, together with the picture moulding of some light wood, will be quite sufficient.

Next to painted walls come the kalsomined or hard-finished walls. These can be agreeably tinted, but are less easy to clean, for they must not be wet. They can, however, be renewed yearly at small cost. If paper is preferred, a simple arabesque or geometrical design is more desirable than a floral one. Papered walls should be frequently dusted with a cloth, which will not only add to the cleanliness of the room, but make the paper look fresher.

The shades should be light in color, matching the wall tint, and if there are draperies besides, these should be either white or pale tinted, and of some thin material, that the

room may have plenty of light. If the outlook is unpleasant or the room near the
street, sash curtains of white muslin, scrim
or madras, in India-silk or the cheaper silk-
aline, will add a certain degree of comfort.
A painted, stained, or hard-wood floor, with
a rug or drugget to deaden the noise of
moving chairs and restless feet, is the ideal
and hygienic floor covering. The paint or
stain should be either dark red or brown, as
these colors have a mineral basis of iron or
manganese, and will wear best, while a hard-
wood floor is most desirable in maple, Georgia pine, or oak. The paint or stain will
have to be yearly renewed, and the wood
floor redressed as often ; but when once
well done, these renewals will scarcely cost
more than the cleaning and relaying of a
carpet.

A dining-room, to be comfortable, absolutely needs a table, a side-table or sideboard, and six or eight chairs. The wood
of all should be similar to the finish of the
room, generally oak or cherry, or pine painted to imitate these woods. At present oak
is the most popular wood, especially the

antique oak which is darkened artificially. Cherry or ash make equally handsome furnishings, and oak and cherry are essentially alike in price; but ash, being out of fashion, is cheaper.

Extension tables are made in two ways. The cheapest, called "stretcher tables," are factory made, stand on four legs, and are strong, their strength and ornamental appearance being enhanced by cross-pieces at a convenient distance from the floor. Small tables three feet and a half wide and extending six feet, cost $8 and upwards, while those that are four feet wide and extend eight feet cost $15 to $20. The narrower width is objectionable, as it crowds the dishes in serving the meals. Although the lesser price is alluring, the wise house-keeper will never buy a table less than four feet wide.

"Pillared base" means supported by a single heavy central post, often braced by four supports connected with the central one. This makes the best of tables, and they come in various grades. Good tables of this sort, factory made, and with ornamentation in turned work, cost from $25 to

$50. They are four feet wide and extend twelve feet. Those whose ornamentation is partly turned and then finished with hand-carving are $50 and more, while in elegant tables with all hand-carving and extending sixteen feet the householder can choose between an oak for $125 and a mahogany for $140.

The standard height for chair seats is eighteen inches, but higher ones for serving at the table can be had at a trifling extra price. The cheapest chairs suitable for a dining-room, and which can be used in a chamber as well, are the square-seated oak ones with caned seats and backs. They are $1.50 each. The "box seat" is the strongest. The term means that the legs or posts are square, and they come through and squarely join in the seat frame, not being turned at the top and driven into the seat frame underneath in sockets. Such chairs with cane seat and back are worth from $2.50 to $4.50 each, according to the fineness of the cane-work and the weight of the frames. Arm-chairs of this sort cost from $2.50 to $4 more.

"Bent wood," which was first introduced here from Vienna, but is now supplied by Western factories, makes the strongest chair frame possible, and at the same time is light and easy to move. The wood is steamed, and then bent and curved. The chairs are made with cane seat and open backs, cane-backed, and also with leather seats. Their durability specially recommends them, though their shape is not so pleasing as that of frame chairs. The wood is either oak or enamelled in black, dark red, or olive, and they cost from $2 each to $6, the arm-chair to match costing a dollar more respectively.

Leather, dark red, brown, or green, is especially adapted for dining-room upholstery, and adds richness to the appearance of the room. Ordinary oak-framed chairs with leather seats cost $4 each, the box-seated being a little higher, and the arm-chair $2 to $4 higher. The seats and backs of such chairs are stuffed with tow and moss, while costly ones have springs and are filled with hair. A chair that will last a lifetime is a box-seated, leather-covered oak one, for which $7 is asked, with $3 more for the arm-chair. But look at the seat! It is first cane-seated, then covered with strong webbing, and finally upholstered in leather.

Another chair which is highly recommended is one with an oak frame for $5 to $9, with the rush bottom of our grandmothers' days. Leather cushions are made separately for $2 each.

Side or serving tables are not only necessary in an elaborately furnished dining-room, but far more in keeping with a modest room than showy large sideboards. They are three feet long, and are fitted with one or two under-shelves, and are convenient for small rooms. They cost from $11 to $16. Next to these come what are called "half sideboards." These have drawers and a cupboard like a genuine sideboard, but are neither so tall, large, nor elaborate. They cost from $14 to $20, and are large enough for the ordinary home. A plain well-built sideboard will cost at least $25, while carvings, bevel plate-glass mirrors, and intricate designs produce elegant and costly ones.

Besides the necessary furniture, there are

other things which add largely to the comfort and tastefulness of the dining-room. If one fortunately has a china-closet or cupboard as an heirloom, no matter what its wood, do not relegate it to the attic, but polish it and give it a place of honor. Its upper part will hold and display the pretty dishes, glass and silver, while the large drawers will hold the table-linen. Even an old-fashioned secretary will do good service in this way, and freshened up with new brass handles, will be another domestic triumph for the "conjuring" housewife. Modern china-cupboards with a glory of bevelled glass can be bought, but the cheapest cost $20, and will not hold a great deal. A better plan, if capacity is desired rather than display, is to have a good cabinet-maker build a cupboard. One fitted to a corner is pretty, and by planning it can be made to contain a double under-cupboard, a drawer for small silver, a glass cupboard for china, and a wide folding-shelf to place desserts on. This will cost $25, but will last a lifetime, and serve for a sideboard till "your ship comes in."

A lounge, leather-covered, is most durable and suitable for a dining-room, but it costs $30. Next best is a couch covered with a rich-toned rug, but this will take $20. A "well-springed" lounge with cretonne covering is better than a hard, showy, tapestry-covered abomination, and will cost but $12. An outlay of $8 will provide a box lounge of domestic upholstering in chintz or cretonne, often described by writers on household topics, but be sure to have the box strongly built by a carpenter and put on casters.

A hanging lamp is the best light for the evening meal where gas is lacking or its price too high, although one may occasionally indulge in the mild radiance of wax candles, and gratify one's pride by using the prized silver, brass, or cut-glass candlesticks. A simple glass lamp with porcelain shade, hung on a sliding rod, will cost $3, while a dollar or two more will buy a prettier one, giving good light. Eight to ten dollars will buy a brass or china lamp of graceful design and fine illuminating power, the well-known Rochester burners coming within this price.

A double spring for the door into the kitchen costs little. The door will swing both ways, and the spring will prevent its standing open. Heat, flies, and odors have less opportunity to make the dining-room uncomfortable if the door is so hung. If the spring is not liked, a tall single or double fold screen to stand before the kitchen door is desirable. A clean kitchen is admirable, but the disorder necessary to meal-getting and other domestic work is not a pleasant sight to accompany every meal, and the fact is that the kitchen door does *not* stay closed. Screens, their varying quality and kinds, will be discussed in detail in another chapter.

Another useful trifle is to line the small silver-drawer with white cotton flannel, first boiling it to remove all traces of the chlorine used in bleaching, or else using the unbleached. Do this, and choose a low-hung drawer—for the noxious gases that tarnish rise—and the needed polishing of the silver will be lessened.

4

VI.

TABLE APPOINTMENTS.

HAVING supplied her dining-room with serviceable, appropriate furniture, the home-maker may now turn her attention towards that attractive part of household supplies, the linen, china, glass, and silver, the daily expressions of domestic refinement, and in whose selection much care, taste, and thoughtfulness must be exercised for successful results. The first thing to be bought is the under cover of table felt. This is wellnigh indispensable, for it protects the table itself from injury by too hot dishes, absorbs liquids when upset that might stain the fresh polish, keeps the linen from cutting through at the edges of the table, besides giving apparent body to inexpensive cloths, and greatly reducing the noise and clatter. This felting is almost the same as double-faced Canton, or cotton flannel, and comes in two widths, one and one-half yards and one and three-quarters. It can also be bought either bleached or unbleached, the standard price of the former being eighty-five cents, and the latter twenty cents cheaper. Both launder well. Though the felting is very durable, a cast-away white or light gray blanket or a coarse worn table-cloth is a fair substitute for it.

The finest linen damask for table-cloths is the hand-woven made in Ireland. It is literally grass-bleached, both the "yarn" itself, as the flax thread is technically named, and the cloth after weaving. Almost equally fine and firm are the Belgian and French damasks, whose cost is the same as the Irish. The finish of the French damask is by far the glossiest, making both table damasks and towels more attractive than the Irish linen at first. Unfortunately, this exquisite finish disappears in the first laundering, never to return, while Irish damask gains in satin-like lustre by repeated washings.

An Irish damask table-cloth and napkins of rarest fineness were shown in New York recently for $87. Pattern table-cloths in

Irish hand-woven linen can, of course, be bought for much less money. From eight to twelve dollars will buy cloths of great beauty and durability, three yards long and two and a half yards wide, but the dozen napkins to match, standard size, three-quarters of a yard square, always cost a dollar or two more than the cloths.

The Scotch manufacturers supply entirely the medium grade of linen in pattern cloths, damask by the yard, and serviceable napkins in standard and smaller sizes. The Scotch linen is not grass-bleached, though the "yarn" of the finer grades is partly so treated before weaving. But the damask, after weaving, is treated to the usual process of chlorine bleaching, which injures the fibre more or less. As a result, Scotch linen "bracks," and does not wear nearly as well as its Irish neighbor. Excellent cloths of good quality can be bought from four to eight dollars each, and the napkins to match from five to nine dollars, both of the standard size. Longer cloths are made, and the price increases from a dollar and a half to three dollars for every half-yard of extra length, varying, however, with the fineness of the linen.

In the best grades of Irish and Scotch damasks the style of designs has changed from the old floral ones to the geometric. Disks, blocks, concentric circles, and waving lines and stripes, wide and narrow, are preferred. Sometimes the design presents broad satin-like stripes, running lengthwise of the table, and on them are laid sprays of flowers of striking form, like fleur-de-lis, in natural size and arrangement. The polka dot of our grandmothers' days — then prettily named "snow-drop" — is still popular, and clover and oak and acorn designs are among the favorite exceptions to the use of geometric patterns.

If the housewife must exercise yet more economy in buying table-linen, this necessity need not discourage her. The Scotch damask made by the yard, of which any amount can be bought, comes in many of the prettiest designs, and the best grade — that sold for two dollars and a half a yard — is fully equal in fineness to the same make of pattern cloths costing five to seven dollars

each. Good quality in bleached can be
bought as low as eighty cents a yard, the unbleached for a trifle less, and when carefully
laundered and placed on the table over the
thick felting it makes a cloth of good appearance. The unbleached and half-bleached
damasks are to be highly recommended, for
they are the most durable of linens in the
medium grades. The fibres are uninjured
by chlorine bleaching and are firm, and the
creamy hue, not unpleasing at first, gradually
passes away with repeated washing and drying in the sunlight. Careful housewives often
buy this linen and bleach it on the grass or
snow before using. It not only lasts longer,
but costs considerably less, in the better
grades, than the same quality of bleached
damask.

But in buying damasks of all sorts by the
yard the home-maker should look well to the
width. A lower price often means decreased
width, and next to the annoying, skimped
appearance of a table with too short a cloth
is that of a cloth too narrow. Two yards
and a half is the best width for general use,
as it will generously cover a table four feet

wide. Three yards is also a convenient length
for the average table, covering it sufficiently,
and not being too cumbersome in laundering.

The holidays, family reunions, and other
festal occasions often demand a long table,
around which all the clan may gather. It is
not always convenient to have a long cloth
reserved for such times, and it is a good idea
to buy two cloths of the same pattern, for
these will clothe the much-extended table
amply, and the central line of meeting may
be easily hidden by a handsome centre-piece,
or by carving-napkin and tray-cloths.

Colored cotton damasks, which can be
bought for seventy-five cents a yard, and in
pattern cloths for three dollars, are entirely
out of use except as economical coverings
for the table between meals. Small diamond
patterns and the old Roman stripes are preferred to the ugly bunches of flowers so long
popular. Lunch and tea cloths have also
lost their colored borders, and the embroidery on them is white. The damasks and
plain linens used for these cloths, for tea and
lunch napkins, centre-pieces, carvers, and
tray-cloths, are always of German weaving,

when they are ornamented with embroidery, either white or in colored silk and gold thread, with drawn-work, or "spachtel-work," otherwise known as Irish point. The Germans excel in these varieties of ornamental work. The linen itself is firm and heavy, but not fine, and sets off the embroidery effectively. Centre-pieces measuring from twelve to forty-five inches square, with "spachtel-work" borders, cost from one to ten dollars, those embroidered all over costing a little less, while hemstitched scarfs for sideboards, buffet covers, and centre-pieces can be found as low as fifty cents each. These ornamental adjuncts of table-covering in moderate homes are usually the work of the nimble fingers of some member of the family. The worker will find this German linen, which can also be bought by the yard or in finished squares and oblongs, best adapted to her needs, and, from its durability, worth the time and labor that must be expended on the work.

Hundreds of years ago, when at King Ahasuerus's famous feast Vashti refused to show her beauteous face, the wine was served in

cups diverse one from another. This ancient fashion of variety in table dishes has
received added impetus during the last few
years, and it not only increases the beauty
and picturesqueness of a well-laid table, but
is a great help to inexpensive buying, while
at the same time it gives ample opportunity
for lavish expenditure. The old fashion of
a complete set throughout for dinner, breakfast, and tea has died out, as a natural result of the revival of decorated china, when
broken dishes, difficult to match, would
quickly destroy the monotonous completeness of "the set." In its place has come
the division into small sets, according to use;
thus, the soup set of tureen and a dozen
plates, the salad set of bowl and plates, the
oatmeal set, the berry set, the fish set, the
lunch set, and tea set (either useful for the
family breakfast and tea), and, lastly, the
roast set.

To buy all these separately and entirely
gives the housewife an array of dishes more
numerous than the old single set, but the
lunch, tea, and roast sets can be bought to
supplement each other, and a reduction in

numbers as well as in cost easily brought about. The conventional roast set consists of twelve dinner-plates, twelve butter-plates, six platters, six casseroles, covered vegetable dishes, six baking or coverless vegetable dishes, and the gravy or sauce boat. This is lavish, and the number can be lessened, or some of the pieces can be used for the fish set, or at other meals besides dinner. The teapot, sugar-bowl, cream-pitcher, slop-bowl, and butter-dish, so long a part of the regulation tea set, are no longer supplied except for country trade. These are replaced either by those alike in china, glass, or silver plate, making a tiny set in themselves, or each can be a different piece, as rare, costly, odd, or rich in coloring as the taste and purse of the buyer may admit. All this makes it possible to be continually adding to one's store. It helps the builder of a new home to begin moderately, even cheaply, without destroying the taste for harmonious furnishings, and gives the pleasure of treasuring each fresh addition and the chance to buy daintier ware than a wholesale first purchase would allow.

"Porcelain" is the ware between china

and the ugly coarse "iron-stone." It is fully as durable as the "iron-stone," and is thinner and more agreeable, refined in tints and decorations, and is the best and prettiest ware for ordinary use. A so-called dinner set in the cheapest grade of porcelain can be bought for fifteen dollars, while those in delicate coloring and dainty shape can be readily found for twenty-five dollars. Such a set makes an admirable nucleus for a service which may be extended *ad infinitum*.

Trenton porcelain is excellent, and comes in all grades and shapes, both plain and decorated in white or cream tint. Wedgwood, an English porcelain, is often seen in blue and white designs, but comes in all colors and grades, some being highly ornamental, while the less costly is usually beautiful in form. Copeland-ware, another English porcelain, has a cream ground, and is generally tasteful in its decorations, while its thinness makes it pleasant to touch without lessening its strength. Thin porcelains are carefully annealed and glazed, so that they do not crack or break as easily as the coarse, stronger-looking earthen-ware.

To have best dishes ready for use when company comes is not altogether so ridiculous as it seems to those who contend that "the best is none too good for the family," and "what's good enough for me is good enough for my friends." Unfortunately the saying that "the pitcher that goes often to the well at last gets broken" is equally applicable to every dish that is in constant use, and it is a comfort in any well-regulated household to know that there are delicate, tasteful, unchipped dishes ready to set before guests, which could not be easily replaced if subject to daily breakages.

Trenton china comes in all grades of fineness, plain and decorated, and a dinner set of it can be bought for about the same price as the well-known Haviland china. The manufactory of this latter china is in Limoges, France, and it produces dishes of great beauty, from the dinner service for fifty dollars to that for fifteen hundred dollars. The gold-banded china can yet be found, but the call for it grows less. In its place is the dull gold irregular banding, the gold flecked, and the tiny edging in gold on raised figures.

Genuine Japanese china does exist, but its price is always high, and the buyer may be sure that the ordinary low-priced "Japanese" tea set or odd bit which attracts her fancy had its birth in New Jersey. Its quaint shape or delicate tinting will add just as pretty a touch to her tea table, however, as if it came "over the ocean." Besides these makes of china, there is "Minturn," which is always nice and satisfactory, while in Crown Derby and Royal Worcester, Royal Dresden, and the rare chinas of Vienna, the house-wife can find ready disposal for all the hundred-dollar checks she cares to invest in them.

VII.

SILVER AND GLASS.

To supply the table with spoons, forks, and knives in solid silver will always be costly, but it gives the satisfaction that, with care to prevent losses, the supply will last a lifetime. There cannot be a great deal of economy in buying solid silver, except in choosing the retail dealer. A few manufacturers of solid silver are widely known, but it is not possible always to buy directly from them, and unless the buyer has friends or business connections in the cities who can direct her, it is far cheaper to buy her goods of one of the reliable makers through some well-known local dealer. He does not have the exorbitant rents of the city to pay, and has a reputation for fair dealing to maintain under the sharp scrutiny of the community, and will sell with a smaller margin of profit than the usual city firm.

All silver is sold by weight, and to the value by weight is added the cost of making. The patterns or designs of spoons and their kindred are numerous, and, with the exception of the most elaborate, there is little increase or decrease in price from them. The plainer patterns are the most satisfactory, as they can be more easily cleaned. In elaborate patterns those that are oxidized keep their beauty longer than those with shining finish, as the background will darken by constant use, and the lost lustre is impossible to regain in the ordinary methods of domestic cleaning.

The average durable weight of teaspoons is six and a half ounces, Troy weight, to the dozen, and they will cost about $11 at retail, while $15 will pay for heavier, finer ones. The regular increased price for increased weight is also reckoned by the ounce at $1.50. While sufficient weight is needed to give strength to spoons, forks, and knives, excessive weight is not an advantage, as it does not materially increase the durability, and makes the articles too cumbersome to handle.

The average weight of dessert-spoons is ten ounces, and that of table-spoons is eighteen ounces per dozen. Both these spoons are sold by the pair, and excellent articles in the former should cost $3, and the latter $5. A butter-knife and sugar-spoon weigh about the same as a pair of dessert-spoons, and should cost about as much, the sugar-spoon being a little cheaper. In forks, the usual and lasting weight is twenty ounces to the dozen, and the retail price is $33 for dessert size, and about $38 for the dinner size. Dinner knives sell for about $50 a dozen, while dessert knives cost from $8 to $12 less. Silver soup-ladles sell for $18, and oyster-ladles for $5 to $7 less.

The prices of single and small pieces of silver, such as coffee, berry, and jelly spoons, fish, cake, and bread knives, and kindred sorts, are fluctuating. They are technically known as "novelties," and the style and selling quality are too much governed by fashion for them to be sold for as narrow a margin of profit as the standard goods are.

While there can be no doubt of the lasting quality of solid silver, there are many comfortable homes, especially new ones, where such an outlay would be often foolish and oftener impossible. And even where a small amount of silver can be had, it is doubtful whether it is best to subject it to the daily wear and opportunities for "mysterious disappearance," from which not the most watchful house-keeping is exempt. There is a great deal to be said in favor of the silver spoon's humble relative, the plated one. This spoon will last from eight to ten years, and look nicely under *wearing* circumstances, will not break, and at the same time takes one care from the over-burdened house-keeper. She can calmly rest, serene in the consciousness that she has her nice silver under lock and key, ready for great occasions, while the thought of rough, careless servants or thieves does not bring a troubled moment.

But to buy plated ware to advantage there are some facts that it is well to know. Forks, spoons of all sizes, ladles, and butter-knives are plated on "albata." This

5

is a mixture of nickel, zinc, and copper. There is said to be twenty parts nickel in one hundred parts of this metallic compound. The manufacturers' catalogues give the grades as " Extra " plate, " Double," " Triple," and " Quadruple." The " Extra " plate is the most sold, and is lowest in price. Each piece is stamped " A1," meaning " albata first quality." The teaspoons are further labelled No. 2, and this signifies that two ounces of silver was used in plating a gross of the spoons. The dessert-spoons and forks have No. 3 on them, meaning the use of three ounces of silver to the gross. Table-spoons and dinner forks are marked No. 4, which means that four ounces of silver plated a gross of them. " Double" plate is double the " Extra," and there are four ounces of silver on the tea, six ounces on the dessert, and eight ounces on the table sizes per gross, and they are stamped 4, 6, 8, respectively, besides the " A1." " Triple" plate is three times the " Extra," and such goods are stamped — teaspoons, 6 ; dessert-spoons, 9 ; and table-spoons, 12 ; and " Quadruple" spoons are stamped 8,

12, 16, respectively, in addition to the "A1" mark, the figures relating to the amount of silver used in plating a gross. Besides these grades there is the triple plate on exposed parts—the tips of forks and spoons, and backs of the bowls and handles where these touch the table when laid down. These are worth about as much as "Double" plate.

The perfectly plain spoon, knife, or fork is richer in appearance in plated goods, but if such plainness is too severe for the buyer's taste, the simpler design will be the better choice. The following is a list of retail prices of the "Extra" grade of plating, the higher grades each costing a little more, and may serve as a guide to the homemaker:

Teaspoons, per dozen $3 00
Dessert-spoons, per pair. 1 00
Table-spoons, per pair. 1 25
Sugar-spoons, each 75
Butter-knives, each 75
Forks (dessert), per dozen. . . . 5 00
Coffee-spoons, per dozen 4 00

All plated knives are plated on steel, and

when the handles and blades are both plated, both are of steel in one piece. Such knives do not cut quite as well as those with bare steel blades, as they cannot be given such a fine edge. They cost $4.50 for the dinner size. Knives with plated blades and celluloid handles cost $10 per dozen for the large size, and $7.50 for the small size. Celluloid does not yellow or crack with age and careless putting into hot water, and is an improvement on ivory, which it has superseded for handles. Knives with steel blades and rubber handles are still to be found. They cost $5 and $4 a dozen respectively, but are a trouble to the house-keeper, as they must be cleaned with sapolio, bath-brick, or sifted coal-ashes after each using.

A steel carving-knife and fork and a bread-knife are yet a necessity, and can be found for $3 and $2 with celluloid handles. Highly ornamented handles of ivory, horn, and mother-of-pearl increase their price proportionately, while prettily cut basswood handles make the knives a little cheaper. These handles must not be soaked in water, but should be wiped off with a damp cloth. Salad forks and spoons are made of bone, ivory, and wood, but are best in wood, olive-wood and Swiss boxwood being the kinds preferred. Plain ones cost less than a dollar, while graceful carving on the handles increases both the beauty and the price.

The best tea service to buy is a plain one with a simple base to each piece. Those with feet as bases do not give satisfaction with long usage, while chased or engraved services lose their beauty because they cannot readily be kept clean and bright. Services do not come in different grades, like spoons, but are all stamped quadruple plate. They are plated on Britannia, a metallic compound of tin, copper, antimony, and lead, which is used on account of its ductility and susceptibility to polish. Plain services retail for $25, and engraved ones from $30 to $35, according to the intricacy of the design. Services are also plated on German-silver, which is an alloy of copper, nickel, and zinc, and cost twice as much as those on Britannia. Solid silver services are very costly, and best suited for use in Castle Bountiful.

Every house-keeper treasures any piece of cut glass that she fortunately has. The glittering heavy glass, reflecting in its prismatic surface countless tints, and sparkling in artificial light with diamond-like brilliancy, adds a touch of elegance which china and silver alone cannot produce. Cut glass is always expensive, as its materials must be of the purest, their melting most exactly done, and the blowing and cutting into the desired shapes manipulated by skilful workmen.

The French cut glass holds the first place by virtue of its costliness and fineness. The English holds the second and the American the third place. It is doubtful if any but a connoisseur could tell why the best American cut glass is not equal to the imported, so excellent has it become. Later years have seen great reductions in the price of cut glass, especially since American manufacturers have competed with foreign makers. There are over a hundred and fifty styles of cutting, but nearly all of them are founded on the old hobnail, rose, and diamond patterns, being largely a combination of straight lines, and the combination being arranged by the fancy and taste of the cutter.

Goblets in cut glass with simplest design can be bought as low as two dollars a dozen, tumblers for the same price, and pitchers for a little more. Berry dishes and carafes, or water bottles, come even cheaper, but these prices are those of the lowest grade of goods. Increased fineness and heaviness of the glass and elaborateness and fineness of the design increase the price proportionately. Ten dollars will buy tasteful fine goblets, berry sets, and the like, while intermediate grades of cut glass produce good effects. It would be impossible to name all the varied cut-glass dishes for table service. The number is great, and the range extends from the tiny salt-cellar and the sweet-toned table-bell to the fasceted centre-piece.

Next to cut glass comes "crystal," which is pressed glass that is more or less cut after the shape and design have been given by moulds. This "crystal" must not be confused with the genuine crystal cut from quartz, and sometimes tinted after cutting. This is exceedingly costly, and is used principally for ornaments. Dishes of the pressed "crystal" can be bought at all prices, and the higher priced are by no means to be despised as a substitute for cut glass. Their design and cutting are tasteful, the glass itself is fine, and each article "rings" with a note of musical sweetness, showing the pure materials of which it is made.

Almost the same may be said of the flood of colored glasses, which are so abundant in all degrees of coarseness and fineness. The material to produce the carmine or red tint is costly, and even in cheapest, ugliest thick dishes raises the price; the blue tint is the next dearer, and yellow, green, and olive the cheapest. Dishes of colored glass, either plain or crackled, with even, delicate coloring, thin and fine in quality, and with a "ring" like a fairy chime when struck, are an artistic ornament to the table, giving the needed bit of bright color as flowers do. The house-keeper can be sure she has expressed herself harmoniously and with refinement if she has bought her finger-bowls

or her cream-jug, her berry dish or odd dishes, of fine colored glass, but she will have to
pay for them nearly as much, and often more,
than for cut glass with simplest cutting or
chasing.

VIII.

UNDERFOOT.

. THE treatment of floors has much to do with the air of comfort which the home-maker strives to give to each room. Carpets *do* furnish, and, so far as " the looks " of a room are concerned, limited furniture and scanty supply of books and pictures will not " go " with stained floors or straw mattings. Such furnishing needs the background of a pretty carpet.

The simplest kinds of wool carpeting are the ingrain and the three-ply. The ingrain has two layers of thread, a warp and a woof, and a good quality is firmly woven and durable. It is capable of endless turnings, breadth by breadth, and changing from the right to the wrong side, being perfectly finished on both sides, though the coloring of the pattern is reversed. All this—its 36-inch width, and the small tasteful designs and subdued coloring in which it is now woven —makes it a satisfactory, economical carpeting. Three - ply, as its name implies, has three layers of threads. These are curiously intermingled, and the design is woven of all three, so that in constant wear, while the upper thread may give way and the design partly disappear, yet there is no hole in the carpet. Three-ply carpeting does not look as well on the wrong side as ingrain, the pattern being brought out less prettily, and although it does not show the floor boards so soon, the loose threads and broken pattern make it shabby much sooner. Both these carpetings have the advantage of being of light weight and easy to sweep and clean, but the best quality alone is worth buying. Of late years carpetings of all kinds have been comparatively cheap, and the best of ingrains and three-ply can be had for 70 cents a yard. A very heavy brand of ingrain, called "Niagara," comes at 90 cents a yard, and is made especially for churches, public halls, and places where severe usage is given.

The next grade of carpeting is the "tap-estry." This is made with a wrong side of linen thread, the pattern being wrought of woollen threads on the upper side. It is 27 inches wide, and although its breadths can change places, it cannot be reversed. A poor quality of tapestry, with the linen bare-ly hidden by the gaudily colored patterns is always alluringly cheap, but is disappoint-ing in the end. The wool top soon wears off, leaving pathways of gray dingy linen streaked around the room, while the flaunt-ing design is a constant torture to the eyes. A small-patterned, neutral-tinted, well-woven tapestry is, on the other hand, a handsome floor-covering, and for those who wish and can have new carpets frequently it is a good investment, while its price—90 cents to $1.15 per yard—is an inducement to those whose money is limited. Tapestry also comes in the same width in all plain dark colors for 90 cents a yard. This patternless sort is called "filling," and is used by many with rugs for rooms where stained or hard-wood floors are not desirable. A room carpeted with "filling" in a dark rich color, and with a large central rug, and other smaller rugs where the heaviest wear will come, has a luxurious air, but is also expensive.

The best carpet for those with moderate means to buy is a "five-frame" body Brussels. Glanced at superficially, it looks like tapestry, but turn a piece over on the wrong side, and the woollen threads will be seen intermingled with the linen ones. For this reason it is impossible for the wool threads to wholly wear off, and so long as the texture of the carpet lasts, it keeps its colors and design. It is the same width as tapestry, and, of course, not reversible. The process of manufacture is identical with that of velvet carpet, excepting that the steel wires of the loom which form the loops on its upper surface are not provided with a knife to cut them as in the case of "velvets." Body Brussels is not only a "five-frame," a technical term from its weaving, but four and even "three frame." These latter have a scanty supply of wool threads and are poorer than tapestry, but they explain the advertisements often seen, " Real body Brussels only 90 cents a yard !" Body Brussels in

freshest design and latest fashion of coloring, and of the "five-frame" quality, will not
be less than $1.35 a yard until the tariff is
removed from carpet wools. The careful
buyer can, however, generally find a limited
assortment of "last year's patterns," or of
short lengths at a reduction of ten to twenty cents a yard. Such carpeting is of the
best quality and safe to buy, while the designs are usually desirable, and sometimes
prettier than those of fashion's latest caprice,
beauty not being confined to the patterns of
any one year.

Velvet carpet, described above as of the
same quality and method of manufacture as
the Brussels, is of wool, as all such carpets
are, but is a trifle higher in price, $1.50, al-
though many pieces can be found, which the
retailer has "marked down to close out,"
for less. Such carpets are hard to sweep
and clean, for lint and threads cling to them,
but are rich in effect, and usually wear well.
Moquettes—a species of velvet of next heavier grade—cost $2.50 and more a yard of the
same 27-inch width; while Wiltons, the next
in order, cost from $4 to $8 per yard. They

enjoy the distinction of being "the best-wearing carpet in the world," and will literally last a lifetime. Axminsters are the most costly carpets, and are made usually from private designs to match or harmonize with ceiling and walls. Such a carpet is woven in one piece to fit the room, and is sold for from $8 to $12 a square yard, the quality sold for the latter price being actually an inch or more in thickness.

In buying carpets of any or all these kinds, the housewife will be better pleased if she buy those of small designs, either arabesque or conventionalized floral, and which largely cover the ground-color, both as a background to furniture old and new, and as a rest to the eye. Carpets so chosen will not become monotonous, and will readily adapt themselves to changes from one room to another. Dark carpets are seldom satisfactory, as they are too sombre, and show dust badly. They are only suitable for rooms of many windows. Light carpets soil easily, and add to the glare of very light rooms, while those of medium tone are best

adapted to wear and to the cheerful furnishing of usual rooms.

Ingrain, tapestry, body Brussels, and all
the grades of velvet have bordering woven
to match. This is priced by the yard, according to its width, which may be from 8
to 20 inches. The buying of a border is a
matter of taste. Square or large rooms look
more thoroughly finished if the carpet has a
border, while in long narrow rooms a border
unpleasantly defines the lack of width. Carpets without borders make over better, and
in rented houses it is undoubtedly better
management to have borderless carpets in
all rooms.

The most healthful flooring is the hard-
wood, or its humbler relation the painted
or stained floor. They do not get full of
dust and moths, and are readily cleaned.
They remove the heaviest load from the
semi-annual house-cleaning, while after con-
tagious illness they do not need special fu-
migating. They are, on the other hand,
expensive from their own cost, and from the
rugs they require to remove the bareness
and to reduce the household clatter. A

house with wood floors throughout is a noisy place where the family is of any size. Hard floors are particularly fitted for dining-room, sleeping-rooms, the library, and music-room; but halls, stairs, and sitting-room are more comfortable carpeted. In the drawing-room a rich effect is more cheaply attained with carpet than with rugs, and the room being less used, its care is less burdensome.

Hard-wood floors are of maple, oak, or Georgia pine, and should be tightly laid and "blind-nailed." The expense varies with locality. Wood-carpeting, or American parquetry, is a recent and successful effort to supply a floor equally as good as a permanent hard-wood floor, but more easily applied. The wood, either walnut, oak, cherry, or any two alternately, is one-quarter of an inch thick, and in narrow strips or blocks, which are glued to a cloth back. The straight carpeting comes 20, 28, and 36 inches in width, and will roll up like oil-cloth, weighing 7 pounds to the yard. Plain borders are made in 3, 5, and 6½ inch widths, and corners, centre-pieces, and strips to form mitre lines

6

come in the various woods. Such carpeting costs from $1.50 to $18 per square yard, that for the latter price being designed intricately with centre-pieces and elaborate borders in oak, cherry, mahogany, maple, rosewood, and walnut. These prices are for the goods uncut and measured before laying, the laying and finishing being separate expenses. Only a carpenter or cabinet-maker can lay these carpets, full directions being given by the city firms that supply them. But carpenters in the country have found trouble in giving this carpet its proper finish, and explicit directions should be secured with the goods. The finish is generally done in shellac, but hard oil or waxed finish is sometimes preferred.

A carpet of this kind, including the laying and finishing, will cost about the same as a body Brussels carpet of the same size, and will last a lifetime. It can be laid over an ordinary floor, and being so thin, doors and thresholds do not have to be cut down. To order it, make a drawing of the shape of the room, showing where are all the windows, doors, projections, and recesses, and carefully measuring and indicating the spaces.

Some floors are too poorly laid to be painted or stained, and the cost of hard-wood or wood-carpeting must be avoided. In such a case "kiddermaster," a heavy ingrain, is an excellent and warm covering. It is a yard wide, alike on both sides, comes in all plain colors, and costs 80 cents a yard. It makes an effective background for rugs, but looks well when used alone.

Straw mattings are a clean cool covering for the floor, but are not durable, which has earned for them the epigram, "cheap mattings are for the rich." A firm, jointless quality, which can be worn on either side, costs 50 cents a yard, and a trifle less by the 40-yard rolls. Cheap mattings split and wear off quickly, besides pulling apart badly. Good mattings are wholesome for sleeping-rooms, and for living-rooms, provided rugs of some kind protect them from severe wear. "Mateline" is a species of straw matting, its warp being a cotton cord, which holds it together better than the usual hempen or straw cord. This is also alike on both sides and seamless, and is sold for the same price.

Oil-cloth, which is a coarse hempen cloth heavily painted, has its uses and its varying widths from 27 inches to $1\frac{1}{2}$ yards. The price also varies from 25 cents to 70 cents. It is especially adapted to back or basement halls and for kitchens, for it is easily cleaned. Linoleum is heavy oil-cloth, durable, but better adapted for offices and public rooms than domestic uses.

Carpet-lining comes by the yard. The best, a double felt paper with a sheet of cotton between, is 10 cents, though by the roll of 20 yards it costs a trifle less. Corrugated paper felting is 3 cents a yard by the roll, and both linings are a yard wide. It pays to put good lining under carpets, the cutting through being avoided and the durability increased. The velvety softness of floors, often noticed in hotels, is due not to the superior quality of the carpets, but to many thicknesses of carpet-lining, five or six layers being often used.

IX.

CARE OF FLOORS AND FURNITURE.

THE best plain staining fluid for floors is permanganate of potash. It acts not only as a stain, but as a disinfectant, and is particularly hygienic when applied to chamber floors. A dark reddish-brown stain is made by dissolving one and a half ounces, costing 15 cents, in a gallon of boiling water. Stir this solution thoroughly with a stick, and put it on with a painter's flat brush, working rapidly, and with the grain of the wood. A smaller brush may be used in corners, and if the stain is not dark enough, another coat can be applied when the first is dry. The stain should then be "set" by three coats of linseed-oil rubbed on with flannel, and with the grain of the wood, each coat being thoroughly dried. Then a polish of beeswax and turpentine should be applied with a flannel and polished with a brush. A brush that is weighted and has a long handle is easiest to manage, but costs $5. Floors so treated stay bright with dusting, but should be polished once a week. The polish is made by covering four ounces of beeswax cut in small pieces with eight ounces of turpentine, and then by placing the covered pot containing the mixture on top of the stove or in the oven to melt. When thoroughly united by the melting, let the mixture cool. It will then be of the consistency of cold cream, and ready for use.

Home-made stainings are largely supplanted by those prepared ready for use which every paint store keeps in stock. The stainings come in cans of different sizes and tints. A pint can of stain is enough for one coat on a medium-sized floor, and costs but 20 cents. When the color is not deep enough, a little lamp-black stirred in the stain will give depth and richness, especially with the cherry stain. Great care must be exercised in using lamp-black, for it is very powerful, a teaspoonful going a great ways, and five cents buying a large amount.

There are many varnishes for sale to apply to stained, painted, and hard-wood floors, and the best general rule is to avoid those that are cheap. They will either fail to dry, or peel up by use and washing. Two coats of varnish, each thoroughly dried after staining, will make a satisfactory flooring that will last a year. Then it may need only "touching up" in the worn spots and revarnishing to be as good as new. Two coats of paint, followed by two of varnish, are also sufficient for a year's wear, and in renewing such a coloring one coat of paint only is needed.

Small portions of paint or staining should never be thrown away, but the can or pail, covered with a paper securely tied on, should be put on some top shelf in closet or store-room or in an undisturbed corner of the cellar, where they will be ready to use again. It is difficult to remix staining or paint to exactly match that already on the floor, and often the whole floor has to be done over for the lack of a little "left-

over " color. When standing has thickened
the staining or paint, a little turpentine will
restore the proper consistency. Most stains,
however, are better thinned with linseed-
oil.

Crockett's filling or preservative, a species of varnish, is especially good on hard-
wood floors, bringing out the color of the
wood and its grain, and being very durable.
It costs $2.50 a gallon, and requires two
coats.

In all painting, staining, or varnishing
there are two secrets of success besides
good materials: to apply each coat with
the grain of the wood, and to let each one
get perfectly hard before applying another or
opening the room to use. Such floors ought
never to be washed with very hot water or
with strong soapsuds, for these gradually
affect the varnish and dull the polish. Oiled
floors are not satisfactory, as the oil soon
dries out, and leaves the wood looking dingy and grimy. For kitchen floors nothing
is so durable as a slate-color. The basis of
this color is white lead thinned with linseed-
oil, and turpentine as a "drier." The color

is given by adding lampblack according to the depth of the tint wished.

In painting old floors the cracks should be filled first. Putty and plaster of Paris wet up with water are used with good results when smoothly laid in with a regular putty or small case-knife. A kind of paper paste, which will harden like papier-maché, is made from newspaper for this use too. Soak bits of newspaper in a paste made of one pound of flour, three quarts of water, and a table-spoonful of powdered alum. This paste must be thoroughly boiled and mixed and the paper well intermingled, till the final mixture is like putty.

Light red and orange yellow are the best colors to use for the backs of shelves in white-wood bookcases. One part of turmeric with thirty parts of water will give the yellow, and a little red turmeric added will give the other shade.

Marble or tiled floors, when not very dirty, can be easily cleaned with sawdust slightly dampened. Stains can be taken out of marble by covering the spots with a mortar made of unslacked lime and very strong lye put on thickly. Leave the mortar on six weeks, and, washing off carefully, rub the places hard with a brush and a strong lather of soap and water. But it is doubtful if oil spots can ever be removed from marble, and all efforts to do so should be made when the spots are fresh.

Straw mattings should be washed with salted water, but wiped dry immediately, as the salt will turn the straw yellow. Linoleum can be polished or waxed like hardwood, while oil-cloth will look fresh if rubbed, after washing and drying, with a cloth moistened slightly in kerosene.

Parquet or wood carpets are finished in several ways. But the first process in all finishes is to sand-paper the floor all over evenly with No. 1 sand-paper. A coat of shellac is then put on, and if the finish is to be in shellac, the floor is again carefully sand-papered after the shellac has soaked into the fibres of the wood and is perfectly dry. A second coat of shellac usually brings out the color of the wood beautifully, and gives a fine lustre. A floor thus finished should have the dust brushed off by a hair brush or a hair broom, or by wiping with a dampened cloth. The floor may be washed with water and a little soap, but must be wiped dry quickly. If the floor begins to look shabby, rub it with a cloth saturated with parquet oil and wrung half dry. Wipe off the surplus oil, so as not to leave any to catch dust. When the shellac is worn to the surface of the wood, sand-paper and re-shellac it as at first, and the wood carpet will be new again. Oiled floors have to be both washed and rubbed with oil more frequently, while waxed floors are cleaned by washing with turpentine and benzine, and then are ready for rewaxing.

Furniture gets dingy, dirty, and scratched with constant use, and should be cleaned and polished at least once a year. Deep scratches or mars will not come out in ordinary domestic " shining up." To remove them the polish must be entirely scraped off with broken glass, as the cabinet-makers would do, and a new polish applied all over the piece of furniture. Pianos and other furniture are polished by the French process, which is a shellac varnish applied with a piece of rubber. A few drops of linseed-oil is added to the varnish itself, and also on the rubber at intervals, till the wood has absorbed all it can. The rubbing is done with circular strokes, and edges and small places that the rubber cannot reach are touched with a camel's-hair brush.

Waxing gives a dull lustre, but scratches and abrasions of a waxed surface are easily remedied. The scratched article must be rubbed with a piece of cork to produce a little heat, and then the wax polish, the formula for which was given in a preceding paragraph, is put on.

Old furniture is polished with a preparation which is made of two ounces of powdered shellac gum, two ounces of copal gum, and half an ounce of gum-arabic. These gums are put into a quart of spirits of wine, and the whole set in a warm place and shaken daily till the gums are dissolved. This mixture should be strained through muslin and rubbed on with a woollen cloth.

Many creams and pastes are used for giving furniture a polish. A good cream is made of one pound of beeswax, four ounces of soap, two ounces of pearlash, and a gallon of soft water, and the whole boiled together till mixed. Equal quantities of beeswax, turpentine, and linseed-oil melted together and cooled make an excellent paste. A furniture oil is made of one pint of linseed-oil and two ounces of alkanet root, heated and strained, and then one ounce of lac varnish added.

A polish for painted wood is made by mixing four ounces of methylated spirits of wine, three drams of oil of almonds, one-quarter of an ounce of gum-myrrh, and one ounce of orange shellac dissolved in warm water. Two parts of linseed-oil, two parts of alcohol, one part of turpentine, with óne ounce of spirits of ether, added to a quart of the mixture, will make a polish equally good for furniture or floors. It should be applied with a flannel cloth, and rubbed into furniture with a piece of chamois-skin or thick felt, and on floors with a polishing brush.

Very dirty furniture can be cleaned by washing with equal parts of water and vinegar, using a flannel cloth. It must be thoroughly and quickly dried, and then rapidly rubbed with a flannel wrung out in linseed-oil. But in applying any or all of these polishes it must be remembered that "main strength" counts for a great deal. The ambitious novice in the household should make haste slowly, allowing plenty of time to the process, and undertaking but few pieces of furniture in one day.

X.

FURNISHING SLEEPING-ROOMS.

IT is not necessary to discuss at length the question of wall and floor treatment in sleeping-rooms. What has been said in previous chapters concerning the hygienic treatment of other rooms applies here with added force. Both floor and wall space should be so treated as to offer the smallest opportunity for absorbing and retaining dirt and dust. If paper is used on the walls, never allow one paper to be put over another. Strip off the old paper first, and then you will see the places that need attention—the damp and mouldy spots, the water-soaked wall, where the bursting of the water-pipes of a previous winter left its traces. Mend, repair, remove these first, for paper, like charity, covers a multitude of sins. But all these evils must be relentlessly uncovered

and removed, else the health of the household is seriously endangered. The kind of
paper used is a matter of taste, excepting
that tints which are light and cheerful are
preferable, and that geometric patterns are
to be avoided. No one knows how soon any
room may be turned into a sick-room, and
then such designs become hideous torments
to the restless, fevered mind and body. For
a similar reason many draperies are not to
be desired. They catch and hold dust and
infection most successfully, and require frequent airing, brushing, and washing to keep
them clean. If the floor cannot be stained
or painted, let the carpet be either straw
matting, or the light but strong ingrain.
Straw matting is sufficiently durable, though
the bed should be placed so that in the
daily making it need not be rolled to and
fro, and, in any event, the casters on all the
furniture ought to be wooden. These are
easily put on old sets of furniture, replacing
the iron ones that left such stains on carpet
or matting, and are always found on furniture of modern manufacture. For hard-wood
floors casters covered with leather, and cost-

ing from 90 cents to $1.25 a set, should be used.

The technical term "a set" of furniture, for sleeping-rooms, means three pieces — the bedstead, dressing-case, and commode. Chairs are rarely bought to match the other pieces, excepting, perhaps, one or two straight ones with cane or rush bottoms. Low rocking or easy chairs in rattan or reed, and wooden chairs with the old-fashioned rush seats, are well suited to a chamber, and give it an air of comfort. Such chairs cost anywhere from $3 to $15, the genuine rattan being quite expensive.

Chamber sets are rarely made of anything but hard-wood, and the painted pine sets, favorites of years past, are seen no more. Cheap beds, chests of drawers, and the like are made of basswood stained or of hard maple. Oak, ash, cherry, and walnut are the woods commonly used. Oak is the most popular at present, and three pieces in it can be bought for from $20 to $125, according to the beauty and massiveness of the wood and the ornamentation, whether it is machine-turned, hand-carved, or a mixture of

7

both methods. The same increase of cost holds in cherry, which rivals oak in popularity, while black walnut, being out of fashion, may be bought for less money in the same grades. The influence of the Eastlake school, with its straight lines, square corners, and mortised joints, is seen everywhere, although its severe outlines have now been modified. But furniture is generally stronger, lighter, and its ornamentation is simpler, and better adapted to ordinary usage than formerly. Curled maple, white-wood, mahogany, and enamelled sets offer every opportunity for indulging in lavish outlay, and can be bought for from $70 to $200. Bamboo sets are a novelty that is beautiful when the other chamber furnishings can be in the same unusual and beautiful fashion, but such a set with an ingrain carpet is wholly incongruous.

Iron bedsteads are unpleasantly suggestive of prisons and reformatories ; but when enamelled and trimmed with brass knobs they are as attractive as they are cleanly. Such bedsteads in full size cost about $15, while a brass one, with its top for a canopy, costs at least $70. A metal bedstead has much to recommend it in its cleanliness and durability, although it has to be draped and kept highly polished to be as pleasing to the eye as the warmer-looking and more usual wood.

Commodes, which are clumsy pieces of furniture at best, are the next article to follow in the wake of the metal bed, and are now also made of that material. Enamelled metal wash-stands of English make are not only artistic, but neat and comfortable. They are of solid metal, but light, and are enamelled in white, and sometimes gilded. The wash-bowl is sunk in the top of the stand, and is usually decorated with a floral pattern in colors. Such stands cost $5, while the toilet set which comes with them costs $8 to $10 more.

The folding-bed is wellnigh indispensable in a city house. It is made in countless ways, to resemble, when folded, about everything from a mantel to a sideboard. It consists of the frame and the spring bed, and varies in price from $5 to $60. One of the cheapest price is called "mantel" bed. The frame is of the lightest description, and the springs of the cheapest sort. The front to the supposed mantel has to be hung with a curtain of some fancy material to conceal the springs in the daytime. The mattress is a separate purchase, and, with the other bedding, is shut in the bed during the day, either folded, rolled, or flat, according to the make of the bed. A thoroughly good fold-ing-bed of hard-wood, with sufficient orna-menting and with accurately working mech-anism, will cost $40, while higher-priced ones present a front gorgeous with bevelled glass and mirrors.

It is conceded that woven wire makes the best spring bed, as it is noiseless, strong, clean, and does not readily sag from unequal weight. Such beds are made in several grades from $2.50 to $7.50, according to the fineness of the weaving and the strength of the wire. The best grade is of closely woven wire supported wholly from the head and foot of its hard-wood frame by coiled steel springs, giving it great strength and durabil-ity. A different spring bed is made of links of coarse galvanized wire hung in the same way, and costs the same amount. Covered springs are rarely made, house-keepers having found that they offer a wellnigh impenetrable hiding-place for vermin and dust. Slat spring beds, which sell for $1.40, have iron circular springs fastened on to pine-wood slats. The slats are liable to break, and the springs "give" in an uneven way that makes a bed uncomfortable. The "dunk" spring is a slight improvement, and costs a trifle more. It is a slat bed, but the coiled springs rest on cords.

There are three kinds of curled hair from which mattresses are made, and all of it comes from the manes and tails of wild horses in South America. That which comes from the tails is called "South American soft" hair; that from the manes, "drawings." The curling is given the hair by twisting it into ropes, and then subjecting it to great heat. This kills all the vermin that may lurk in the hair, and further strengthens its curly, springy quality. The black color is obtained by dyeing, while the gray is from gray horses and by partial bleaching, and the white made so by vigorous bleaching.

Forty pounds is the standard weight of a mattress, and made of the "South American soft" hair, and covered with the time-honored blue and white striped ticking, it costs $20. Such a mattress will last a lifetime, and furnishes a luxurious bed. The "drawings," which is harder and more springy hair, sells at retail for 70 cents a pound, while gray or white hair is 60 cents. Gay, fancy-striped ticking increases the price of the mattresses, but, though pretty at first, this fades. Different and elaborate ways of tufting and finishing the mattress increase the price. One filled with gray hair, with its case made with eyelet-holes and laced with a cord, may be had for $70. Such a mattress can be unlaced at home, and then the hair "picked up" with the case still on.

The amount of dust which works into a mattress is scarcely comprehended by the house-keeper, unless she sees it as it flies in clouds when the hair is cleansed. This dirt, unhealthy in all ways, cuts the hair and injures it. Mattresses should, consequently, be renovated as often as every four years. This costs $2 in the city, and in the hands of a reputable house the work will be well done. Cases to cover mattresses are valuable to prevent this dust working in, as well as the soiling of the ticking. Such cases, ready-made, cost $3, but are less if the housekeeper can make them herself. It requires about ten yards of single-width holland, silesia, or unbleached muslin for one. Mattresses are easier to handle when made in two parts. The division is not made exactly in the centre, and the smaller part is placed at the foot of the bed.

The third kind of hair is "South American soft," mixed with pig hair, and is called "mixed hair." This is made in three grades, respectively, 45, 40, and 35 cents per pound, the last being mostly pig hair. But although this mixture of pig hair lessens the price of a mattress, it is poor economy to buy it, for it mats and wears out in a few years, and cannot be renovated satisfactorily. Indeed, the only reliable and healthful mattress, besides one of genuine hair, is one of husks, with a layer of cotton next to the ticking. Such a one, costing $5, does not mat easily, is light, and the husks can be taken out and washed, and, when thoroughly dried, be packed back in, making the mattress fresh and clean.

Many things are used as substitutes and adulterants for curled hair in mattresses and upholstery. Gray moss that grows on trees in the Southern States is one. It is gathered and desiccated, dyed, twisted in ropes, and then baled. When shipped to Northern markets it reappears as "vegetable fibre," "African fibre," and "Japanese hair." A kind of tall marsh grass, growing along the banks of the Niagara River, is used in a similar way, and although the moss and grass are not hurtful, yet no one cares to buy them as curled hair. Mattresses made of these and of excelsior, with a cotton-batting top, are fairly comfortable. Hair does not make a good top layer for these cheaper substances, as it will work into them, and soon the hair top is conspicuous by its absence. Wool is little used for mattresses except in France. House-keepers do not wish for them, as the wool is likely to be adulterated, mats and grows hard, and is heavy to handle.

Pillows are sold according to weight, and when made of live-geese feathers will last a lifetime, and can be renovated many times. The standard sizes and their weights are 30 inches by 30 inches, 5 pounds ; 26 inches by 30 inches, 4½ pounds ; 22 inches by 30 inches, 3½ pounds ; 20 inches by 30 inches, 3 pounds. The prices are 80 cents a pound for a good article called " live geese," and $1.25 for the choicest, "imperial feather." These latter are the "live-geese" feathers carefully picked over and every quill removed. There are many sales of feathers at cheaper prices, but these are invariably largely mixed with hens' feathers, and are a "dear bargain," though the cheap grade is useful for domestic upholstering.

XI.

SHEETS, BLANKETS, AND TOWELS.

WHEN the necessary furniture of the bed-rooms has been bought, the housewife must turn her attention to the judicious buying of the bedlinen. Years ago, when our grand-mothers spun and wove their household stores themselves, linen sheets were the rule and not the exception ; but now the reverse is apt to be the case, and "cotton is king." In hot weather and during illness the cool, soft surfaces of linen sheets are more com-fortable, and every house-mother justly prides herself on having a few of these textile treas-ures.

Linen sold for sheets and pillow-cases is wholly grass-bleached and of Irish or Bel-gian weaving, unbleached linen for such uses not being imported. Its width is ordi-narily ninety inches, and it costs from eighty-

five cents to $2.50 a yard, according to the
quality of the linen, its weight and fineness.
The width for pillow and bolster cases is
forty-five inches, and its price forty cents to
eighty-five cents.   Linen in narrow widths
can be found, but the widths given are
the standard measures.   Linen sheets, hemstitched, of Irish make, are sold for from $5
to $12 a pair, and the cases to match for
from $1.75 to $3.   Those with a slight pattern of embroidery along the hem are $14 a
pair, and the cases $4.50, while sheets of
beautiful quality, with both hemstitching and
embroidery, cost $12 to $15, and the corre-
sponding cases $3.50 to $4.50 a pair.   These
are as dainty and luxurious as the most
fastidious could wish.

Muslin is now universally used for bedlinen in the ordinary home.   There are
many mills which supply an excellent article,
and muslin comes in varying widths to suit
all sizes of beds.   The quality for durability
should be firm, and the thread coarse rather
than fine, although the latter seems desirable
at first.   The unbleached muslin is preferable to the bleached for the same reason, as

the bleaching process impairs the textile fibres. The half-bleached recommends itself as a division of the evils. It whitens rapidly in frequent washings, and wears nearly as long as the unbleached. The sheet with a seam up its centre has been discarded, thanks to the helpful looms, and remains only a bitter memory to those who spent weary hours doing their daily " stent " upon their seams. Such sheets were never wide enough, as the muslin was but a yard wide, and the sewing was a tiresome waste of energy.

Muslin that is ten quarters wide is the best width for a full-sized bed, the nine quarters being a generous width for the three-quarters bed, and the 45 to 50 inch muslin for single beds. There are from 40 to 50 yards in a piece of "sheeting," as it is technically called, and a good quality in unbleached nine quarters wide costs 20 cents a yard, while the less durable but attractive bleached is 8 or 10 cents more. The narrower muslins are not generally so firm and heavy in texture, but a good grade of the 42-inch width can be bought for 12 cents, unbleached, and the bleached for 3 cents more. The prices of half-bleached muslins are midway between those of the bleached and unbleached, and the cloth has the soft finish, an agreeable feature to the sewer.

A sheet should never be less than two and a half yards long, as nothing is more annoying than a sheet which pulls out at top or bottom. When the wide seamless sheet grows thin in the middle, the thrifty housewife tears it apart, and neatly and quickly hems the raw edges on her machine. Whether she sews the selvage edges for the middle seam also by her machine or over-sews it by hand depends upon how deep in her nature sank the instructions of her youth. "Union sheeting" is a compromise both in price and material, being half linen and half cotton thread. This is not commonly sold, and is only woven in standard widths for sheets and pillow-cases.

Every blanket that is all wool is now called "California," although the original ones so designated were woven of California wool. The price of wool blankets depends upon the weight, which averages from four to six pounds for a good article, and upon the width. This is measured by quarters; but although the blankets are woven of honest width, the process of "fulling" or finishing shrinks them so that to have a blanket measuring actually nine quarters one must buy one marked ten or eleven quarters. Good all-wool blankets of eleven quarters, the average width, and weighing four pounds, will be $5, while $8 will buy a finer one. The prices increase with increased weight and width, till one marked thirteen quarters and weighing six pounds will cost from $12 to $15.

White and gray cost the same price for the same quality, but scarlet ones are a trifle more expensive owing to the dye. This latter color is not much sought in the finest grades, and is not kept in stock, although it may be relied on as always all wool, the dye quickly showing the cotton if mixed in. Another advantage in the scarlet blankets is that they do not readily soil.

The cheap grades of blankets in gray and white are made of mixed cotton and wool carded together, and so skilfully is this done

that it is difficult to tell when a little cotton
is put in. Such blankets in medium sizes
are from $2.50 to $3 a pair, while that mis-
nomer a cotton blanket is but $1.50. Small
blankets for cribs and cradles come in all
but the cheapest grades, and are rarely anything but white. They cost from $2 up to
$8, the latter being soft and downy enough
for the little princess of fairy lore whose
sensitive flesh felt a single bean through
ten mattresses and ten feather-beds!

Although the " throw-over," *couvert de lit*,
as the French have it, made of lace and lined
with silk or satin, is undeniably the most
artistic way of dressing a bed, its very beauty
makes it both too fragile and too costly for
comfort in the average home. The time-
honored Marseilles spread is the best for
general use, and now comes woven in white
and dainty pink, blue, buff, green, and cheerful scarlet, as well as all white. The colors
are fast, and the laundering is not a difficult
matter, as the spreads require no ironing.
They look far better smoothly folded and
put under a heavy weight overnight. Light
spreads of this kind cost as low as $2, while

$15 marks the extreme of beauty in design and fineness of weaving.

The machine-crocheted or "Bates" spreads are much liked, and can be worn on either side, besides being less stiff and clumsy to handle in washing. Such spreads are woven in all grades, and are sold from 75 cents to $2—so cheap that even those with limited means can have their beds daintily clothed in snowy white. Irish hand-crocheted spreads, made of linen or cotton coarse thread, are handsome bed-coverings. They are made of both bleached and unbleached thread, and the patterns are highly ornamental. The spreads are finished with a heavy fringe, and to show their full beauty should be lined with silesia of some bright tint. Such a spread will cost $5 for a single bed, and for a full-size bed from $8 to $15.

The aristocrat of the family of comfortables or puffs is the eider-down duvet. The duvet is very light and soft, and when covered with India silk costs $15, and is truly a regal affair. Others, covered with French satine or challi, are less in price, varying from $6 to $10, according to size, quality of the down, and the covering. Although these duvets are expensive at first, their lightness and durability make them a good investment for the House Comfortable.

Comfortables made of cotton wadding can be bought from $1.50 to $8. The quality of the cotton, the kind of covering, and the tying (whether done by machine or by hand) affect the price. The cheap ready - made ones sold at the shops are never desirable, and it is a mistake to buy them. They are usually made of waste cotton, and are heavy and "lumpy." Home - made comfortables are by far the best. Soft textiles, such as satine, cheese - cloth, cotton or wool challi, make better coverings than calico, which was thought indispensable years ago. "Butter-cloth," which is cheese-cloth forty inches wide, is excellent for such a use. None but the best cotton—which may be had for fifteen cents a roll, and a roll weighs a pound, should be used. Three pounds of cotton is enough for a heavy "puff." Fifteen yards of cloth three-quarters of a yard wide will make a comfortable two and a half yards

8

long and two and a quarter wide, the average size, and when firmly and closely tied it can be washed as often as need be. Comfortables are not to be recommended as the regular bed-covering. They are, however, invaluable for the extra supply which must be stored away in summer. The voracious moth, which your best blankets will attract, will leave the cotton puff untouched.

When *couverts de lit* are used pillow-shams are dispensed with, for the *couverts* are large enough to cover pillows and all. Many house-keepers prefer linen shams, and these can readily be bought. The linen is of German weaving, and those finished with simple hemstitching sell for from $3 to $12 a pair. Fancy shams with embroidery or drawnwork are $4 to $10, as the linen used for them is a trifle lighter in quality. Beautiful shams, with hemstitching and spachtelwork upon them, are also imported from Germany, and are from $10 to $12.

The durable and perhaps best towel for every-day use is the "huckaback." The peculiar weaving gives the towels unusual absorbent qualities and sufficient roughness to

be a mild irritant to the skin. All huckaback towels are of Irish make, the finer ones
being grass-bleached. Three to six dollars
will buy a dozen of excellent quality, while
$15 is the price of a dozen fine ones of ex-
tra size, and with a border woven in satin
damask. In the damask towels there are
those of French, Irish, and Scotch manufacture. The finer grades are generally
hand-woven, measuring one and a quarter
yards long by three-quarters wide, and, as
in the case of the table-linen, the appearance of Irish damask towels improves with
laundering. Those which are hemstitched
are from $12 to $18 a dozen, and of beautiful quality. Towels with knotted fringe are
$10 to $15 a dozen, but the hemstitched
edge is preferable, for fringe wears off and
requires extra work in ironing. French damask is a little heavier, and a dozen towels
of it cost from $12 to $24. Scotch fringed
towels are of lighter, coarser weave, but are
good for common use, and excellent ones
are $10 a dozen. Turkish towels are woven
of both linen and cotton, the former being a
fine article. The cotton towels are 30 cents

apiece for those of full size, and the linen are from 40 cents up to $1.25 apiece, the latter being almost a bath-blanket. Towelling which comes by the yard is called crash. Cotton crash, which is rarely worth buying, sells as low as 6 cents, while the linen varies from 7 cents for fifteen - inch width to 25 cents for the twenty-seven-inch width, the latter being fine and heavy.

XII.

CURTAINS, SCREENS, DRAPERIES, AND RUGS.

THE tasteful dressing of the windows has much to do with the outward appearance of a house, and yet more with the inner aspect of each room. The first requisites are the shades. These are usually made of holland —a kind of stiffened linen—and hung upon weighted spring rollers. The best holland is the Scotch, while the cheaper grades are included under the term "painted." Shades can be bought in all tints, from white to dark red, but the medium tints of gray, buff, and olive adapt themselves to the general coloring of most rooms. White shades soil quickly, holland does not wash, and white does not darken rooms agreeably when the shades are drawn. Some artistic Queen Anne houses have neither inside nor outside blinds, and in such a case it becomes necessary to have two sets of shades, a dark green next the window and the tinted ones inside. Holland comes in varying widths, and is usually sold in window lengths of two and a half yards. The price, including the rollers, is from 60 cents to $1.25 a window, but the cheap grades are not worth buying, for the holland fades quickly, and shrinks and wrinkles with the least dampness. Extra lengths and widths cost more proportionally. It is economic as well as good taste to buy all the shades of one color. Shabby ones can then be easily replaced by new, and worn ones relegated to less conspicuous windows.

The selection of the drapery curtains gives a wide range wherein to exercise one's taste within the limitation of one's purse. The economical way of buying materials for sash and long curtains is to buy only such fabrics as will wash, or those that from weight and color never require it. There are many wash goods to choose from—the old-fashioned but always dainty tamboured or embroidered muslin, the dotted or striped Swiss muslin, India silk, the genuine madras, and scrim. These can be bought by the yard; and neatly hemmed or hemstitched, and further trimmed by little ball and tassel fringes that come in both colored silk and white cotton, will all make neat, pretty drapings for the windows.   India silk for draperies is thirty inches wide, and from 80 to 95 cents a yard. Dotted and embroidered muslins are a yard wide, and cost from 20 cents upwards, while real madras, both the creamy white and the figured and colored, is the same in width, and from 30 to 50 cents a yard.   Scrims, plain and fancy, are from 10 to 25 cents a yard, but in buying both them and the other wash draperies abundant allowance must be made for shrinkage, else one will be annoyed with "high-tide curtains" after the first laundering.

There is a bewildering mass of cheap fabrics for such uses, and occasionally colors are fast.   These cheap goods frequently answer the purpose where durability is not an object, but their freshness and bright tints disappear in a few weeks if used where the sunlight pours upon them.   In such materials may be classed the printed madras, the silkoline, an imitation of India silk in cotton, and the colored scrims. None of these are over 15 cents a yard.

Few rooms are well lighted enough to bear dark heavy curtains, and the general use of these, except in rooms exposed to severe winds, gives a gloomy, morose effect to the home. And in the excepted rooms heavy hangings are not pleasant save in winter when the cold north wind creeps in at the casement. Drapery curtains of embroidered muslins, Irish point, scrim with antique lace insertion and edge, are admirable, and hung upon either wood or brass rods, and looped back with ribbon or chains, give an air of refinement to any room. They are sold in pairs, and the average length is three and a half yards. The muslins cost $5 to $15, the Irish point from $5 to $28, the tambour lace $5 to $35, and the scrim from $3 to $10. The colored madras which drapes so gracefully in soft folds comes from $3 to $25 for a pair, and is not only harmonious in its coloring, but never requires washing, the latter fact being the great disadvantage of white curtains. The madras should be hung out-of-doors to allow the dust to be blown out, and then should be pressed on a blanket. Nottingham lace still survives, and is sold by the yard and in pattern lengths, but it is out of favor, and justly so, for it is as inartistic for window-hangings as cotton imitation lace is for the neck of a well-bred woman's gown.

Screens are of indisputable value in household decoration, and, in addition to their ornamental qualities, they are useful as well. In chamber or dining-room, in drawing-room or nursery, they are always acceptable. Among the cheapest are the Japanese paper screens. Large ones, four feet high and with four folds, cost $3.50, and those six feet high cost $6. These have enamelled cloth backs, making them durable, and the smaller size cost proportionally less. The Japanese screens with embroidery in gold thread on black silk and with bamboo frames are beautiful. Those four feet high and with three folds cost $4, while those five feet high and four folds cost $8 or more, according to the intricacy of the design. Unmounted screens are made of cherry, oak, hard maple, ebonized wood, enamelled wood, and bamboo, so that a screen can match the prevailing wood in the furniture and finish of each room. Such frames cost from $2.50 to $10, the price depending on the height, number of folds, and the spindlework which ornaments the tops. Teak-wood screens are rare and costly. Mahogany screens with embossed leather covering are rich, and suitable for an elegantly equipped dining-room. Single screens to place before a fireplace are generally of bamboo with gold embroidery, and these cost $5. Stained-glass single screens framed in brass or wrought-iron are particularly beautiful, their bright colors glowing before the fire-light, and they cost from $15 up to $50.

Materials for mantel draping and covering of screens are so numerous that only a few can be named, which may serve as guides to the home-maker in her purchases. Chintz, printed sateen of twenty-four inch width, and costing from 12 to 25 cents, and silkoline, are adapted for decoration in chambers; India silk, stamped velvet, and velours, the latter two being $1.50 a yard, are suitable for drawing-rooms and library, while plush with its soft pile lends itself harmoniously to rich decorative effects. Scarfs for the mantel, the easel, and picture-frames should be of some soft clinging silk or gauze, and the fancy-stores and woman's exchanges supply a multitude of dainty trifles for this use, while nimble fingers can fashion many at home.

The same bewildering variety of fabrics may be found from which to select portières. These, like screens, are both useful and ornamental in nearly every room. The comfort and spacious appearance of a home is increased by them, while if not too lavishly used they are a graceful addition to tasteful rooms. Turkoman portières, which are a mixture of cotton and wool, or jute and wool, are sold in all plain colors banded with fancy borders, and are serviceable. They cost from $2 to $5 each. Chenille portières have a soft velvety finish and richer coloring. They sell for $5 to $25 each, while portières of velours, a heavy silken fabric, are $25 to $300. Countless fabrics of Oriental design and coloring, and sometimes the actual product of Eastern looms, are admirable for hangings, and vary in price. Japanese bead and bamboo portières are unique for decoration alone, and are of moderate price, averaging about $4 a pair. The old-fashioned blue and white woven counterpanes make quaint portières. They should be ripped apart at their centre seam and then hung singly, the fringe forming a border.

The ingrain rugs were originally called "Woodstock," after the English town in which they were first woven, or "Kensington Art Squares," from the art school which supplied the design. Now they are made in American factories, and one nine by twelve feet can be bought for $10. The genuine "Woodstock" rugs are imported and more expensive, one two by three feet costing $4.75. Such rugs are light and easily handled, and are particularly suitable for chamber use and over carpets and mattings. Kazak and Daghestan rugs are woven on hand-looms. The Kazaks are made in Turkistan, among the Caucasian Mountains, and have a short nap. One four feet by seven feet is $50. The Daghestans are of nicer quality, and are made higher up in the same mountains. They range in price from $10 to $50, according to size. These rugs are not alike on both sides, while the Smyrna rugs, made literally everywhere, but the genuine ones in Smyrna, are alike on both sides, and especially serviceable on this account. Small ones of American make are less than $1, but those with soft coloring and firm texture cost from $5 to $45, the latter being 9 by 12 feet. There are other Eastern rugs which are more costly, but they belong more suitably in Castle Luxurious. Woven rugs should not be shaken or whipped on a line, but laid on the grass and beaten with a rattan beater.

Japanese rugs are of cotton dyed in dull colors, and are principally used in temporary summer homes. One three feet by six costs $2.50, but the colors fade rapidly, so the buying of such rugs is not recommended. Fur rugs give warm, luxurious effects, and all kinds are for sale, from the little red fox-skin, with its head mounted on, to the lion-skin, the most expensive of all. White, gray, and black bear-skin rugs in moderate size are $3 to $8, leopard rugs $20 to $50, and tiger rugs, with the fierce head mounted at one end, cost $100, and often more.

XIII.

THE FAMILY HEARTH-STONE.

No room in the home so perfectly typifies the communism of a family, the true uniting in diversity of the individuals, as the sitting-room. It is the centre of the social life of the household. It is "mother's room." There she is oftenest found in her moments of leisure, ready to hear, to sympathize, to console, and to advise. Here the father frolics with his children; here they listen to song and story read aloud; here the troubles of the day dwindle and disappear, or are softened and lessened by united sympathizing and soothing surroundings; here nuts and mild jokes are cracked, and rosy apples and fragrant oranges lend their flavor and juicy richness to the homely scene, while without the wind blows, the rain falls, or the snow flies.

To make this room the ideal hearth-stone, its furnishings should contain elements that appeal to the tastes and pursuits of each of the members of the household.   There should be room, if possible, for favorite chairs and for shelves or bookcases, and tables for each one's choice of books and papers, and for undisturbed corners and cosey nooks, if each has only a chair and footstool, or portion of a drawer, or a curtained shelf.   Places where the studious, the ambitious, or the thoughtful can work out their pet projects, or keep safely their treasured plans and possessions, ready for the sudden inspiration or the industrious mood, which quite as often seizes one amid the family chatter as in the solitude of one's own room.   To secure all this will require considerable outlay as well as much unselfish thought on the part of the home-maker. The outlay, however, can usually be modified, adding purchases from time to time as family growth and taste may show them to be desirable.   Indeed, the true furnishing of such a room, after a certain point, must be a matter of growth.   Given the bare bones of chairs, carpets, tables, and curtains, the rounded form and vigorous expression of the sitting-room must grow out of the mental and moral life of the family, grow out of that social, intellectual, and spiritual food on which the family feeds. Of course furnishing selected with this aim in view will be as varied as families are, for what expresses comfort and gives help and solace to one family would be tiresome, inane, or comfortless in others. Each home writes its own history sooner or later in its furnishings and arrangements. Even straitened means—that oft-berated foe of family luxury—cannot prevent the telling of the tale. Year by year slips by; purchase after purchase is made; chapter after chapter is written. What we most desire we bend our circumstances to secure, and therefore the home does express in the long-run what we are and what we feel. This being true, let us not be impatient; let us proceed thoughtfully, unselfishly, and carefully, that our home centre may not express sordid lives, ungenerous natures, or narrow minds.

The home is for the family and not the

world, and there should never be a moment's hesitancy if narrow means compel the furnishing of but one room—a parlor or a sitting-room.   Let the sitting-room come first. It should never, on the other hand, be the receptacle of broken-down or useless drawing-room furnishings. . Good plain articles which are yet honorable in their strength and usefulness can frequently be put into the sitting-room when the state of the family finances has allowed something handsomer to be bought for the drawing-room. Too often the sitting-room receives but rickety tables, cracked ornaments, spotted upholstery, and chairs whose springs are warped out of any comfort-giving properties they may once have possessed.   So, in bringing any furniture from the parlor to the sitting-room, let the housewife see to it first that it is restored to strength and rendered clean and inviting in all ways.   " The best is good enough for my own," should be her watchword, not " Anything for us, and our finest for our callers."

Again, the hard-wood or parquet floors with a warm, large rug and smaller ones

9

scattered around in needed places is the best floor coverings for the sitting-room. These floors have been described in a previous chapter, as well as the rugs, so mere mention of them is sufficient. If a carpet must be used, a body Brussels is the most serviceable; and one whose coloring is neither light nor very dark, and whose design "does not rise up and strike," will give the most lasting satisfaction. Next to the Brussels, the ingrain may be chosen. It should be well lined throughout, and carefully laid. Extra breadths of carpet lining placed where the wear will be heaviest add greatly to the durability of any carpet, especially to that of ingrain. If an old carpet must be used, it should be carefully cleaned, ripped apart, and remade, so as to bring the least worn parts in the centre of the room, and to place the shabby spots in retirement in the corners or under large pieces of furniture.

The coloring of the wall, whether by means of paper, paint, or kalsomine, should be made to harmonize with the carpet, repeating or contrasting with its lighter tone.

The wood-work is best treated when it is simply left with its natural color and grain brought out and protected with a coat of shellac. Cherry and walnut are the most satisfactory of stains, and if paint is used almost any color is better than white, which shows every finger-mark and every worn spot.

In the selection of draperies the housewife should be chary. Such a room needs some adornment, to be sure, but these airy, graceful trifles are a vexation when more than sparingly used in a sitting-room. They gather dust and lint to a fearful extent in a constantly used room. Where there are plenty of house-maids there can be plenty of draperies with hygienic safety; not every woman can give the time daily to the slow, fussy task of dusting each textile fold and loop. But whatever draperies are chosen, let them be thoroughly good of their kind. In the family sitting-room the sunlight must stream and the fresh breezes blow; but these bring destruction to poor fabrics and fading dyes.

A fireplace or coal grate is an important

part of good cheer, and is the best ventilator, and should be in every sitting-room if possible. The furnishings of a fireplace are the andirons, fender, screen, stand of tongs, shovel and poker, and the brush and bellows. A complete set of these in brass will often cost $50, while a less elaborate set can be bought for half that sum. Each article can be bought singly, and the outlay be thus made gradually.

Wrought-iron andirons are from $3 to $5, and the fenders from $5.75 to $11. Nickel fire-sets are of medium price, while the brush and bellows, sold together, are from $4 to $7. Brass coal vases are from $5 to $14, and brass scuttles are from $5 to $7. Coal vases of japanned metal are from $2 to $7.50. These vases are designed for the use of cannel-coal, which comes in large lumps, and is placed on the fire with tongs, but they are awkward to pour the usual hard or soft coal from. Bronzed-iron fire stands are $2.50 a set, and are sufficiently good for the ordinary home. Baskets to hold wood for a fireplace are from $3 to $6.

When a fire on the hearth alone will not

heat the room sufficiently, and there is no furnace or steam heat to be relied on in cold snaps, it is better to have a good stove. It is never healthy or comfortable to be chilly, and when one is cheated into half-warmth by a hearth fire one joins heartily with the Western poet who sang, " The land of stoves and sunshine is good enough for me." Cylindrical stoves take up the least room, and sell from $3.50 to $15, while the art square stoves are more ornate in design, and cost from $8 to $75. The linings of these stoves are cast-iron, which is the best, and even the lowest-priced stoves are fitted with all the ingenious dampers.

A couch for the sitting-room, well up-holstered in raw silk, will cost $10 to $35 ; one covered with a Turkish rug, $16 to $35 ; and a cretonne-covered couch costs $10 to $15. These prices seem high, but such a piece of furniture gets severe wear, and it is poor economy to buy a couch or lounge that is not "well sprung." Velvet is the durable fabric for upholstery, but raw silk is the most used for re-covering furniture. It has but little silk in it, however, being a mixture of wool and cotton, and costs from 45 cents to $1.25 a yard. Jute is a strong, cheap fabric, but it fades badly. Both raw silk and jute come fifty inches in width.

A " set " of furniture is neither desirable nor fashionable, and in the miscellaneous furnishings so common now none are more comfortable and lighter than those of rattan or reed. An arm-chair in rattan costs from $5 to $10, while smaller chairs are from $3 to $8, and sofas $10 to $20. These all need cushions of velvet, silk, or cretonne, which add to the gay aspect of the room. The mother's comfort is added to if some one buys for her a pretty work or sewing table, which sells as low as $5. A large table with billiard-cloth top makes an excellent · centre table, around which all can gather. Such a one costs $12, while a table with folding top costs $14. Smaller tables of oak or cherry can be bought for $4, but in this room the table should be at least four feet square.

Cushions for foot-rest should not be forgotten, but they are usually of home manufacture. The substitutes offered by the shops are hassocks. These are made of either tapestry or velvet carpeting, and good ones cost $1. Cheaper ones are poorly made and filled with shavings, which soon leak through the seams, for hassocks are not lined.

XIV.

THE KING'S DOMAIN.

A ROOM for a nursery is almost a necessity in a household where there are young children. It not only separates them from the rush and hurry of the adult life of the family, which is a severe strain on the nervous force of young children, irritating and confusing them to an extent greater than is often understood, but it gives the parents an opportunity for quiet, rest, or social diversions. These are needed, for the calmness and patience demanded in the care of children cannot be maintained by parents when the nerves and muscles are "all of a quiver" from ceaseless childish demands. As it cannot be the House Comfortable without baby voices echoing through it, let us make the special abiding-place of the little ones cheerful and pleasant, and, above all, a place of safety.

A room with windows opening to the south is the best for the nursery. While this cannot always be commanded, one with a northern outlook is to be avoided. Such a room is cheerless, cold, and unhealthful. A chamber is also better than a ground-floor room, as it is less likely to be damp, and the floor will be much warmer. Great care should be taken with the ventilation of this room, where children are to spend so many hours, and it should not also be used for a sleeping-room when such use is avoidable. If this cannot be avoided, the room should be opened, aired, and rewarmed before "the sand-man's visit." In windows with medium-sized panes, removing one of the higher panes and inserting in its stead a pane of tin with a circular ventilator in it is an excellent way to secure fresh air in houses not provided with fireplaces or ventilators built in the chimneys. A pane of glass can also be set in a slight frame and hung on a pivot in the sash in the centre of its top and botton. This will allow the pane to be moved, swinging open sidewise, and a cord fastened to the pane by a small knob or screw will enable one to open it without reaching.

If the room is warmed by a stove, its size should be adapted to the room, keeping it neither too warm nor too cool; and great care should be used that the dampers work perfectly, and that the draught up the chimney is good. A plain cylindrical stove is preferable to an "art stove," as it offers less angles to hurt when toddling feet fail in their duty, and less shining nickel to tempt restless fingers to their burning. Such stoves with cast-iron linings are now sold for from $5 to $15, while the pipes and elbows are a separate expense, which varies according to the amount needed. Stovepipe is sold by the foot. The "Russia" pipe, which has a fine lustre and is more durable, costs three times as much as that of common sheet-iron.

Nurseries should never be papered, unless a coat of varnish is afterwards applied. There is great risk of using a paper whose coloring contains arsenic. It becomes soluble in the air, and is an acute irritating poison to the throat and lungs. Besides, children are peculiarly subject to infectious diseases, and in such a case the room must be disinfected. The only way to disinfect wall-paper is to remove it. Paint, which can always be washed and disinfected with little trouble, is the most healthful wall-covering. It can be kept clean always, and, once on the walls, will last for years. A bright warm tint should be chosen, cream-color, buff, pink, light brown, or terra-cotta being among the prettiest. Next to paint is distemper-color or kalsomine. This is healthful and clean, and though it must be renewed every year or after an infectious illness, this can be done at small expense. Distemper can be tastefully tinted, but it is best to use with it a dado of paint or varnished paper, because kalsomine comes off when touched or rubbed.

The first point to be noticed concerning the nursery floor is to see that the doors, especially the outer door, close tightly. A crack at the threshold lets in a constant draught, and little children who sit on the floor get many a cold as a result. So, if you please, plenty of cracks overhead, but none underneath door or window. A loose creaking board may cost a mother many an hour of extra labor with a nervous, wakeful child, so see to it that such nuisances are gotten rid of, a hammer and nails being an effective remedy. Hard-wood or staining is doubtless the sanitary treatment for the floor. But the bumps and blows from falls upon the wood are severe, and sanitation by their use is quite too Spartan for most mothers.

The best carpet for the nursery is one of ingrain, well lined and securely nailed down. Such a carpet is easy both to sweep and to clean. Oil-cloth and straw matting, although easily cleansed, are objectionable. The oil-cloth is too cold, and straw matting will break off in tiny fibres. These work into the clothing and almost ruin it; and, worse than that, the particles pierce a child's tender flesh, and make painful slivers. Large rugs of ingrain, such as the "art squares" or "Woodstock rugs," which are as large as the room, are good, but small rugs are a constant snare for little feet, and should not be tolerated in the nursery. A fur or sheepskin rug is delightful for a frolic, but when the play is over, it should be carefully put away.

As the nursery is also the play-room, furniture should not be so abundant as to crowd the playthings. Leave plenty of space for the doll-house, the rocking-horse, the blocks, and trains of cars. The table should be of medium height, with rounded corners, and steady on its legs. If an old-fashioned table with leaves is used, see to it that the bed of the table is broad enough to balance the leaves when they are leaned upon heavily, as is sure to be done. Casters on such a table add to its tendency to tip over, and should be removed. Broad shelves set on brackets at the windows, or hung on strong hinges to fold down when unused, are a great comfort for little people, and are an inexpensive addition.

The only rocking-chair in the nursery should be the mother's, and that not a patent rocker, with its metal spring ready to cruelly pinch unwary fingers. It takes a good many years to teach a child not to stand in a rocking-chair, and little straight or " steady " chairs are much safer for children, saving them many falls, and the care-taker many a fright.

When a lounge can be added to the furnishings, a home-made box lounge, with its top cushioned by a mattress, is more serviceable than one from the upholsterer's. The mattress will bear jumping on better than springs, while the box will hold childish treasures. Denim, which is a twilled cotton, and comes in dark blue and brown, both plain and striped with white, is strong, and makes the best covering for the lounge and its big pillows. Its colors are fast, which is not always true of cretonne. In fastening on the denim flat-headed nails alone should be used, and the corners of the box be well cushioned. The box lid ought to have a hasp or hook and eye to fasten it open, lest the lid drop suddenly on a small prying hand.

Another need in the nursery is low-hung shelves on which a child can place his books and especial toys, and some low hooks in closet or wardrobe where he can hang his own coat and cap. It is useless to expect orderliness and self-helpfulness in a child if we do not give him the means to learn them early and in the care of his own possessions. Proper care of books, clothing, and toys cannot be taught too soon. Learned in babyhood, such traits become an instinct, and do not lessen the happiness then or in later years.

A shelf on which to place a clock and the medicine which one may be giving temporarily, is indispensable, and should be hung high, beyond the reach of the most active climbing child. Where gas is not used, a hanging or bracket lamp is the only safe one. A plain hanging-lamp will cost $3, while a bracket-lamp may be bought as low as $1. There are many little lamps and tapers for burning during the night, and almost any kind can be bought for less than a dollar. The dainty fairy-lamps, with their delicately tinted porcelain shades, are really candles, an especially thick short candle being made to burn in them. The German night tapers are curious little contrivances, and perfectly odorless. They are sold by the box by wholesale druggists for four cents, including the float of tin and cork. One of these tiny tapers will burn all night when placed on the float in cotton-seed oil. Any shallow dish will answer to hold the oil, which sells at wholesale for eighty cents a gallon.

Besides spirit-lamps for nursery use, in which alcohol is burned, and which cost from fifty cents to $1.50, there are several arrangements for utilizing the heat of a gas flame or a kerosene lamp to warm water or milk in the night. A gas-burner with its end shaped like a disk, and pierced around the edge with tiny holes, costs fifty cents. A cup or small basin of water placed on the disk after the ordinary burner has been un-screwed heats quickly. One can be perma-nently fastened on an unused nursery or bedroom burner, and will be found a great convenience in cases of sudden slight illness or at odd times. For lamps a wire frame is made which can be inserted in the top of a lamp chimney. It raises the tin cup suffi-ciently above the top of the chimney to pre-vent the flame from smoking. The heating is, of course, a slower process than by the gas flame. A quarter of a dollar will buy one of these frames or a tin chimney. Such a chimney should be made to fit the burner, and have a flaring top cut in scallops. Near the top it should be perforated with several large holes to serve as air-passages. A cup or basin can then be set on the chimney's top.

10

XV.

"SHE MAKETH HERSELF COVERINGS."

WHENEVER it is possible to have a room set apart for the family sewing it will be found a great convenience, and in a short time a genuine necessity. The sewer can do her work more readily when all the materials are at hand, and the work can be left in any stage of progress without being put away for fear of meddlesome fingers or unexpected visitors. It adds considerably to the labor of the housewife if she tries to sew in her sitting-room, dining-room, or chamber, for the "picking up" and "putting to rights" take her steps, time, and energy, and usually when she is tired out with successes with her needle and shears.

A sewing-room need not be large. Inbeed, a small room is better, for it keeps the tools and materials of the sewer easily at hand.   In city houses the hall bedroom is an excellent one for such a use, and if it be on the north side of the house, so much the better.   The north light is the best to sew by, and the room will be cooler for summer tasks.   A furnace will keep the room warm in winter, and if stove heat is all that can be had, the small room is easily warmed from an adjoining one.   The dress-maker who makes periodical visits to the ordinary home likes a room to herself, and the family aversion to her presence is lessened if she herself is not immediately visible.

The floor should be a bare one, stained or painted, or—the nearest approach to such— covered with matting or oil-cloth.   Threads, bits of cloth, and the lint and dust from reno- vating old garments cling to wool carpets, and make a sewing-room one of the hardest to sweep.   To brush up such litter and then wipe the floor with a dampened mop is a short, easy task.   The curtain should be merely a shade, but capable of rising to the window's full height, that all the light may have free entrance.   During the winter a long curtain of Canton flannel may be hung on a rod over the shade, so that the north wind cannot come whistling in at the loose window if the mending - basket calls the housewife there evenings. Such a curtain should reach the floor, and in plain colors, or figured patterns alike on both sides, will cost from 15 to 25 cents per yard.

A low rocking-chair is the easiest to sew in, and it may be of rattan, wicker, or wood, as the buyer may fancy. Rattan is the most costly, and while the American rattan-work is finer, the chairs are not so well shaped as those of Chinese or English workmanship. Chinese chairs are usually a mixture of rattan and wicker. A rattan chair will cost from $5 to $10, while a comfortable wicker chair may be had for $3. A rush-bottomed, hard-wood rocking chair without arms, such as have so long been popular on piazzas, makes a cheap, excellent sewing - chair. Cushions of feathers, or even excelsior covered with chintz, cretonne, or denim, for the seat and back, make it quite luxurious, and are easy matters of home manufacture. This denim is an old friend under a new name. It is really bedticking, but is woven a trifle finer out of respect to the decorative uses to which it is now put. It comes in plain dull blue, plain brown, blue and white, and brown and white striped, and is firmness itself in texture.

An ordinary chamber chair is also necessary, to use when working at the table. Much cutting and basting can be done at a table, and quite as easily if the worker is seated. The table, which may be a discarded one from the dining-room, should be lower, perhaps two inches, than a dining-table, that the sewer may not be fatigued by having to hold up her arms while working. This table should be at least three feet wide and four or five feet long—a size well adapted to cutting out cloth of differing widths, and casters should also be supplied to move the table easily. Small cutting-tables come with folding legs, so they can be "reduced to lowest terms," and occupy little space when not in use. These are virtually standing lap-boards. They cost from $2 to $2.50, and are made of narrow strips of light and dark wood, one strip being marked off in inches and fractions like a tape-measure. Regular lap-boards come made of similar strips of hard-wood, and cost $1.50. They are durable, but heavy to hold, and for that reason one of paper or felt is an improvement. Such are of light weight, are metal-bound, to keep them from warping, and they cost less than a dollar.

Besides the sewing-machine, whose use is almost universal, a well-equipped sewing-room needs a scrap-basket, a rag-bag, piece-and-pattern bags, a chest of drawers, and, lastly, a hassock or footstool.

In no other room in the house is it wise to attempt home carpentry, but articles of general utility and comfort made for this room do not get the severe strain on their weak joints which things for every-day house-hold wear receive at the hands of the family. The scrap-basket is one such. It can be made of a discarded peach basket, tea-chest, or other box, provided it is firm and un-broken in the start. Cover the basket in-side and out with cretonne or denim. Line the tea-chest or box with paper or cloth, carefully pasted in, and exercise your dex-terity in either case in fastening on the outer flouncing, and you will have a receptacle for scraps just as useful as a $3 one of good basket-work, and fully as durable as a cheaper reed or splint one. Even an empty butter firkin, dried, cleaned, and painted inside and out, will be well disposed of if it finishes its career as a scrap-box.

Bags for patterns, pieces of clothes, and rags should be made of denim or strong cretonne, calico and gingham not being strong enough. The sewing - room can be made to look neat if the house-keeper is able to make these, her chair cushions, and box coverings all of one kind of cloth, matching the prevailing color of her heavy winter curtains. One yard deep and three-quarters of a yard wide is a good size for piece and rag bags, while pattern-bags should be half as large. Two bags are better than one for pieces of the family clothing—one for woollens and the other for cottons — and they should be hung in the sewing-room rather than in a closet, where it is troublesome to get to them, and where they crowd clothing. One rag-bag is enough. Since paper is now rarely made of rag pulp, the rag-bag is no longer a valuable source of "dicker" for bright new kitchen tins. A basket to hold patterns can be made of a large grape-basket, either painted all over or lined and flounced to match the scrap-basket.

Better than bags for the pieces of clothing and the patterns are cabinets. Such cabinets can be built of pine, with or without backs, screwed firmly to the wall, the bottom not more than a foot and a half from the floor, and stained or painted, "as you like it." For a family of four to six a cabinet four and a half feet wide, four feet high, and one foot deep, which will give four rows of three pigeon-holes, each hole about eighteen inches wide by twelve inches high, will be of ample size. Each member of the family can have two pigeon-holes allotted to her and labelled with her name, one for cottons and one for woollens. The two which would be the share of the father can be devoted to miscellaneous pieces of household textiles or for patterns. The front of the cabinet can be closed with a curtain, but doors are better.

If the room where the cabinet stands be

narrow, its doors should slide instead of swinging open. The best sliding doors have two parallel grooves in front of the pigeon-holes. In the inside groove stand two doors, each covering one-third of the front. In the outside groove is a door a little wider, so that with the two inner doors pushed to the ends of the cabinet, the outer door will cover the space between them. Then the doors can be pushed so as to expose any pigeon-hole desired. Such a cabinet must be made by a carpenter to be satisfactory. It will cost about $5 with curtains, and about $8 with doors. The readiness with which any bundle can be found or put away will make the cabinet a constant comfort in a busy family. If a piece of fresh tar-paper is kept in each pigeon-hole, the female moth will se-lect less fragrant quarters to lay her eggs in.

A footstool can easily be contrived from a small wooden box, and covered to match the scrap-basket, if one does not wish to buy a hassock. An old-fashioned chest of draw-ers or an unused bureau is a necessity to the orderliness of the sewing-room. New ma-terials and garments already cut out will fill one drawer. Garments in process of making and old ones for remaking and mending can be put in another; while the yarns and cotton for mending, the small basket or work-box, with its needles, threads, and scissors, can be conveniently placed in yet another drawer. Here, too, will be the labelled boxes of extras, threads, braids, tapes, buttons, and countless little trifles so often needed. A small well-covered board to do pressing on, needed by every capable sewer, and its companion, the holder for the iron, should also find a resting-place in a drawer. A flat-iron and stand can also be added, while a one-burner oil or gas stove, standing on the top of the chest, will provide the worker with every needful tool ready to her hand.

XVI.

PICTURES FOR THE HOME.

NOTHING grows by what it feeds on more rapidly than the love of beauty, and for this reason every home should have a few good pictures, at whatever cost; and fortunately cheap and good process reproductions of fine pictures are not beyond the shortest purse. Good photographs are also cheap, and are artistically the most satisfactory reproductions of a great masterpiece. Good pictures one must have, as one has books, for their educating value. As between books and pictures it is sometimes difficult to choose, but as between either and fine china, draperies, or any luxurious decoration whatever, there ought not to be an instant's hesitation. Children reared in the atmosphere which good books and pictures give can hardly fail to absorb refinement from their surroundings, and, after the sterling virtues, no quality is more desirable.

In selecting pictures for the home, several other qualifications besides their artistic value must be taken into consideration. First, the wall space of drawing-rooms and living-rooms is usually limited, and only comparatively small pictures can be hung there to advantage. Yet the drawing-room picture, to be effective, must show its full value across the room, a distance of from three to a dozen yards. For this reason pictures crowded with small figures do not show to advantage in private houses.

There was at one time a fashion for hanging in parlors and halls engravings of American historical pictures involving many figures. The patriotism of the custom was admirable, and the engravings were excellent, but the effect was bad, because the portraits of the historical figures were so much reduced that the features became indistinguishable unless one stood before the engraving and studied it—which is not what home pictures are for. If one wishes patriotic pictures—and every home should have a few, as it should have the American flag to hang its "banner on the outer wall" on the Fourth of July and other national days —single portraits of great Americans will be found more satisfactory than pictures where many of them are combined.

The same thing is true of pictures selected wholly on artistic grounds. A large reproduction of one or two heads from frescos of the old masters is more effective than a photograph of the same size which includes the whole group. Fortunately there are enough single figures of immortal beauty, of which there are excellent etchings and photographs, so that no one need be troubled in finding good material to ornament the walls of her home.

Trouble comes from the fact that poor pictures, or, at best, pictures with only a superficial and evanescent charm, are reproduced as freely as the good. A superficial book has this great advantage over a superficial picture, that after one reading the covers close and need never be opened again. But the superficial picture hangs upon your wall, to be seen daily, until at last the repetition

of its emptiness becomes so oppressive that
it is banished to a chamber, or torn from its
frame and something more satisfying sub-
stituted. Bear this in mind, especially in buying pictures of children. Hundreds of them
are painted and reproduced which either tell
a pretty childish story or catch some phase
of childish " cuteness," whose charm is for
the moment only. Test the childish picture
that has caught your fancy by the " Penel-
ope Boothby " or the " Miss Bowles " of Sir
Joshua Reynolds, or by the cherub heads of
Raphael or Murillo. Any picture that will
bear such a comparison has beauty enough
not to wear out its welcome too speedily.

There are landscapes which reproduce the
poetic beauty of the scene that suggested
them, and whose effect does not depend
upon a clear outline of details. Some reproductions of these masterpieces, particularly in etching and process work, preserve
the beauty of tone of the originals, and these
are most welcome additions to the walls of
the home. Figure pictures, to the exclusion
of landscapes and marines, are a mistake.
They even become tiresome, and the eye

longs to see the calm refreshing portrayal of nature in her varying moods offsetting the passion and power of pictured human nature.

As to oils, by all means have them if you can have good ones, or even one good one. No possible decoration is so greatly to be desired. But a fine etching or a photograph of a great picture is infinitely better than a dauby or a commonplace oil, which is a veritable apple of Sodom. There is one class of oils, however, in which really good work is not very costly—flower, fruit, and still-life pieces, which are attractive on drawing-room, sitting-room, or dining-room walls. Delicate life-like clusters of flowers are always a delight, and their restful influence and dainty coloring are akin in a minor degree to the effect of a peaceful landscape, whether they are executed in oils or water-colors. This latter medium—whether used for landscape, marine, or flower pictures —is refined and agreeable, and pictures done in it are not beyond the reach of ordinary purchasers. But they should be bought with careful thought of the places they are to occupy on the walls. Water-colors need strong light and a near view to bring out the fine details, excepting those pictures which are pronouncedly of the "impressionist's" style of execution. Such ones need a strong light but a somewhat distant view, as details are intentionally merged into massed effects.

A picture may be well chosen, but its framing may neutralize its effect and render it a distracting object. Hence the buyer's care must not relax or her taste and sense of the fitness of things be "off guard" till she has selected her frame. A frame should never be more striking than the picture. It should accent the picture, and yet in itself be unobtrusive. It should soften the lines of the wall around the picture and focus the eye upon it.

Oil-paintings should be framed in gold, silver, or bronze. A frame of white and gold is best for a water-color, while engravings and etchings look best in frames of natural wood, either polished or varnished, but never gilded. Photographs can be framed in natural wood or modest flat gilt or bronze frames, according to the subject and the

tone of the picture. Soft gray or cream-
tinted mats are the best for pictures in general, throwing the picture back from the glass
and softening the effect, but tinted mats may
occasionally be used. A dark blue mat, when
the picture is blue in tone, or a wine-colored,
or rarely a silvered or gilded one, may be
very effective, but should only be used cautiously. The frame for an oil-painting should
never be flat, but always thicker at the outer
edge, to throw the picture back and increase
the perspective in which it is best seen, and
harmonize it with the walls. Sometimes an
oil is of modest coloring and low tone, and
is most effectively framed in dark crimson or
dull blue velvet, the pile of the velvet softening the picture yet imparting a luminous and
rich effect, which the glitter of a golden frame
almost wholly absorbs to itself.

Water-colors are very often harmoniously
framed in tints which carry out the delicate
prevailing color in themselves, especially in
landscapes and marines. The mat can often
be the palest tint of cream, pink, buff, atmos-
pheric gray, or sea green; while the frame
itself may repeat the tint, with delicate lines

11

of gold, or be made of simple white and gilt moulding.

The gilded frame is delusive, often being nothing but the cheapest imitation in plaster of Paris thinly gilt. This soon drops to pieces. In good gilded moulding there are two kinds worth buying. The French is costly, and has two layers of gold-leaf and a coating of lacquer varnish. This will last a lifetime. The German moulding has a single coat of gold-leaf, and then the varnish. It is less costly, and will last many years.

A word may be said in regard to hanging pictures. They should be hung so that the centre of the picture will not be more than five feet and a few inches from the floor. This is the average height of a woman, and enables one sitting to see a picture with the eyes naturally and slightly raised, while one standing has his vision directly opposite the heart of the picture. Very large pictures may be hung a trifle higher, but the same general proportion must be observed. A picture at such a height may be hung nearly flat against the wall; but in hanging a picture over a tall piece of furniture or another picture, select one of vigorous outline and bold execution, and tip it forward several inches from the wall. Very small pictures should be hung low, and are best treated in groups of three or four. Sometimes such small pieces are more decorative than artistic, and their brilliant coloring is then seen best over a large, sober etching or photograph. A small picture that is at the same time fine in its details and execution should be placed on a little easel on table, mantel, or shelf, where its artistic daintiness can be seen at once.

In choosing a large picture for an easel to "break up" a bare corner or awkward space, do not select a single-figure piece or a bold, strong landscape. The position on the easel throws the picture into greater prominence than those on the wall, and, by contrast, the picture itself should have a finer and more detailed subject. A fine landscape or a group of small fine figures invites attention, and bears well the scrutiny which placing on an easel gives it.

XVII.

THE POWER OF COLOR.

No other single element adds so greatly to the beauty of a home, and therefore to its comfort, as the skilful use of color. If one is so fortunate as to be furnishing a room from the beginning, wall-paper, curtains, and carpets that harmonize, with drapery, wall banner, picture-frame, or chair cushion of the appropriate bright tint to properly accent the duller masses, cost no more than a heterogeneous collection of furnishings, each one bought for its own special attractiveness, without regard to its harmony with the other fittings of the room. Moreover, any one who starts for the first time to furnish an empty room in this way, with a trained eye for harmony in color, will pause midway in surprise. She has not put into her room all she supposed it needed, or

all she intended to buy, and yet, behold! it
looks furnished already.

A sense of warmth and richness can be
produced by the proper use of warm-tinted
hangings, which cannot be equalled by lavish and expensive if inartistic ones.   Every
reader will recall rooms beautifully yet cheaply furnished in this way.   The writer has a
vivid recollection of a transformation so
wrought in a large square room.   Unfur-
nished it had not one redeeming feature.
There were eight doors, grained in a yellow
imitation of oak after a hideous by-gone
fashion, very little wall space between the
doors, and two long casement windows opening upon a piazza which shut out the sunlight.

The woman who expected to make a sitting-room of that place had very little money
to spend.   She put upon the walls a cheap
paper of a rich chocolate brown, with a pattern of straggling roses in dull yellow, a narrow frieze with a dark red flower in it, and
a band of dark red velvet paper underneath.
That done, the glare of the yellow doors was
perceptibly softened.   Then the floor was

painted a dark brown, and an ingrain drugget of graceful pattern in cream, black, and
red was laid in the middle. On this was
placed a cherry dining-table with spindle
legs (descended from a grandmother), both
leaves raised, covered with a cloth in dull
red and black, and supplied with a shining
student-lamp and a litter of books and magazines. The only available pictures were
some unpretentious flower studies in oil in
narrow frames of polished oak.

The most expensive chair in the room
was a $5 wicker rocker run with red ribbons.
There was a bookcase of pine stained brown,
and in this were some handsome books, and
on it some pretty vases. There was a clumsy
home-made lounge stuffed with excelsior and
cotton, and covered with cretonne, also in
brown and red. The deep windows were
hung with long brown Canton flannel curtains, with cross bands of scarlet, hung on
two mop handles, " ebonized " in a carriage-
painter's shop in fifteen minutes. The whole
outfit, except the books, vases, and table, had
not cost $50. Into that room went friends
of all degrees of culture, from the art-school

graduate to the village blacksmith, and they united with substantial unanimity in the opinion of a boy of ten, who, having been sent there on an errand, went home exclaiming, "Oh, mother, they've got the boss room up at the —— !"

Another simple combination, even more effective than brown and red for a room which is well lighted, is pearl gray and a lighter red. Nothing else has quite the warm effect of a heavy brown or dull red curtain, but pictures stand out exquisitely on a gray wall, and the simplest line of color doubles its value against such a background. For that purpose a plain gray paper without a pattern, or with one wellnigh invisible, is best, and the frieze should be of a dark red. With a shaded gray carpet threaded with a scarlet and dark red vine upon the floor, a few etchings or photographs upon the walls, and some pots of blossoming plants, even if nothing more than the hardy scarlet geraniums, such a room will radiate cheerfulness. It will absorb all the glittering ornaments it can get, and metal or cut-glass vases or shining silver candlesticks are a great addition. The ideal high light is given by an open wood fire burning on brass andirons, with a polished brass fender. Gray walls hung with handsome etchings and engravings are more beautiful without the scarlet frieze for those who do not crave color. But most uneducated eyes· long for this brightness, and the average man sympathizes with the fireman who wanted his engine painted " any color, so she's red !"

More subtle than either of these, and more difficult to manage, is a harmony of pale gray-green and terra-cotta. Such a scheme of decoration was effectively used in a well-lighted double drawing-room, with its walls covered with pale gray-green cartridge-paper, its frieze of a graceful floral design in terra-cotta, and its ash woodwork shellacked to show the grain of the wood. A Brussels carpet, with an arabesque pattern in black and white on a terra-cotta ground, and chenille patternless portières repeating the soft green tints, continued the restful coloring. Most of the furniture was in cherry, with here and there an oak book-case or rocker, and a daintily silvered rush-bottomed reception chair. The chair seats were in plush, either terra - cotta or gray-green, with one or two in deep crimson accenting and enriching the calm beauty of the coloring. Cream white Irish guipure drapery curtains on gilt rods, and tastefully chosen etchings, engravings, photographs, and water-colors in modest gilt, oak, and cherry frames, added the finishing cultivated touch of harmony. The furnishings were indeed all handsome, and somewhat costly; but the result was one of artistic loveliness, uncluttered with bric-à-brac, suggestive and restful, and one which money, even in much larger amounts, could never attain alone.

The first two of these suggestions are simple outlines of effects within the reach of the least experienced home-maker. The last requires a more artistic eye for the effective arrangement of the color tones. Given an artistic eye, there are limitless refinements and subtleties possible in the combination not only of two colors, but of three or four or half a dozen. The great point to remember is that color counts, and not to throw colors into such association that each neutralizes the other.

The real difficulty of getting a satisfactory color effect is not met by people who can furnish one or more rooms newly from the start, but by those who must use things they have already, and add to them one or two pieces at a time. Under such circumstances it becomes difficult to give a room unity of design, and to buy to-day the chair or wall-paper that shall not put out of countenance the sofa or the carpet of ten years ago. The first thing to be done is to discover what tone your present belongings have, if any, and what tone you can introduce which will harmonize with the greatest number of them. For this reason carpets and wall-papers selected singly should be dull in tone and unobtrusive in pattern, and the same is true of the covering of upholstered furniture. Rugs, portières, window-curtains, and mantel draperies should be selected as much for their color as for other qualities, and, deftly chosen, may be relied on to brighten up an otherwise commonplace room.

A handsome rug with a preponderance

of dull blue in it, laid before a mantel hung with drapery of paler blue, above which is a picture in a gilt frame, with heavy dark blue portières in another part of the room, and with a blue vase or two, and bits of gilt or dull red against the pale blue, will give distinction to a room the various belongings of which have no special color harmony.

In such a room it is not necessary to remove everything which does not fit the color scheme to a nicety. Nature harmonizes all sorts of colors in small space, and many diverse shades can be satisfactorily put into the same room. In out-of-door harmonies the colors of leaf and flower are seldom vivid, the brilliant effects being produced by masses. There are textile blues, greens, and reds so vivid as to kill everything with which they come in contact. Furniture or hangings of this description will always be an eyesore. But if your old furniture is in dull tints, it will not look any older or more shabby for an artistic use of color in new belongings that are put with it.

Of course no general rule can be laid down for color treatment of partly furnished

homes.   Each interior is a problem by itself,
to be worked out by its occupants.   But, as
a guide which personal taste and circumstances may qualify, it may be laid down
that a library should be dark and rich, a
dining-room bright in coloring, your sleeping-rooms as near white or creamy tints as
possible, and the drawing-room in cool yet
bright effects.

In the use of browns and greens several
grades of the color, shading into each other,
are desirable, as they make a less monotonous effect, and harmonize old and new belongings better.   Shades of red are more
difficult to use, and red, as the chief color
of a room, although warm and rich, is apt to
be unrestful; but to lighten dull masses red
and yellow are invaluable.   Bright shades
should be used sparingly, but a little gold
embroidery may be as grateful as a vase of
flowers in a room full of rich browns, and a
little crimson or pink satin or velvet will
brighten effectively a room whose prevailing
tints are browns, greens, or dull blues.

XVIII.

WITH PIPE AND SLIPPERS.

EVERY house should have one room where the husband and father can smoke without fear and without reproach. No room in a house is such a comfort to the "gude mon" as his "den," when he can have one. Here, watching the smoke curling up from his cigar or treasured pipe, he can meditate lazily over things in general, or, with slippered feet toasting before the fire, mentally settle perplexing questions away from all the jar and clatter of the domestic machinery. The occupant will not be critical as to its size or the locality of the den, so it will be quite easy to devote any room which can be most readily spared, be it on the ground or chamber floor. A northern outlook, few windows, or an unattractive view will matter little if the creature comforts and tastes have been considered.

Such a room is more frequently used in winter than in summer, and with the exacting claims of business life, is rarely sought except in the evening. The effort, then, must be to make a warm-looking room, whose coloring and furnishings by their richness and cosiness express the idea of restful quiet. An ideal room of this sort, which can be modified as taste and circumstances may suggest, can be attained with simple yet tasteful arrangement in dark golden brown, with traces of scarlet as high lights, for this is one place where dark coloring is effective and suitable.

Stain the floor dark brown or cherry, and over it place one large rug, Smyrna, Turkish, or ingrain, as the purse may permit, carrying out in tone the two colors chosen to be the key-note of color harmony in the room. If this is not liked, fur rugs—two or three—in black or gray, give a look of warmth and luxury, and are a great addition, especially if it is necessary to use a carpet. At the windows place heavy hangings in brown, with a scarlet pattern or design upon them. The double-faced Canton

flannel adapts itself nicely and cheaply to
such a use. The plain color with bands of
scarlet appliquéd on is effective and lights
up brilliantly, while some figured design is
frequently as desirable.

A fireplace there should be in the ideal
room, and a corner one, too, whose cheerful
blaze will give especial charm and add zest
to the reveries of your own pet and particular Benedict. To such a fireplace brass
andirons and fender, mirroring the danc-
ing firelight, are a fitting accompaniment.
Brass andirons cost from $9 to $15, and the
fender $5 to $17 ; while the scuttle, and the
stand of tongs, poker, brush, and the little
red leather bellows, add from $15 to $38
more to the bill. If brass is not liked, and
its brightness and beauty require much laborious rubbing, nickel or wrought-iron can
be the metal instead. Fireplace furnishings
of these metals, bought new at the shops,
are often as costly as those of brass, but
old ones sought out in some garret or junk-
shop, or one's own heirlooms, can be cleaned
and restored from their shabby estate, and
made to do brave service again. But if

there is no fireplace, by all means get that excellent substitute, an open stove. These come in several different makes, with much shining nickel and tile ornamentation, or severely plain, and for $6 or more you can have one that will do its work cheerily for years.

If there is no mantel, make one. A broad pine shelf, firmly supported on brackets and fastened on the chimney wall of the room, will answer very well. The board can be stained like the floor, or covered with Canton flannel or any other fabric taste and means may suggest. Then make a gay lambrequin in brown and scarlet, and fasten it on your shelf, hiding the supporting brackets. This lambrequin will furnish a wide field for choice in its design, material, and the fancy needle-work upon it, and will be a much-appreciated place for loving fingers to sew in their thoughtfulness and attention, because Benedict likes pretty trifles when not in his way. Now on the mantel-shelf put as pretty and unique a tête-à-tête tea set, with its creamer and sugar-bowl, as you can buy. If your own fingers can decorate it, choosing some favorite flower for its design, or you can guide the fingers of "our daughter" in her efforts to paint something for papa, so much the happier and better. Besides the tea set, you will want to place with it a Russian samovar and spirit-lamp, a pretty tray for use as well as to make an effective background to the bright brass kettle. A pretty dish or basket to hold crackers and fancy jars for tea and prepared cocoa must be added to complete the mantel array. Your Benedict will prefer that his dreams die not away in smoke and ashes, but rather to see them realized with your own face opposite his while you make "the cup that cheers" for him and any other friend who may chance to be admitted to the privacy of this room.

The chairs should be easy and comfortable for the most part, with a couple of upright, light bent-wood or framed chairs besides. Leather makes the most durable and suitable covering for both the chairs and the indispensable lounge or couch. The leather should be either brown or dark red, and when well upholstered the lounge will

12

cost $28, and an easy-chair $15. But such an outlay not being possible, the home-maker can often utilize some old worn pieces of furniture which were originally well made and are yet strong. These can be re-covered, or, if that be yet too much expense, neat covers of cretonne or chintz in harmonizing colors can be made at home, and slipped over the shabby upholstery.

A table will be next in order. Be sure that it is of generous proportions, large enough for writing upon, for a game of whist, or for the magazines, papers, and books, whichever may be the chief pleasure of the owner of the room. Such a table may be a cheap one with a deal top that $3 will buy, or a plain hard-wood one for $10 or $12. In either case a table cover will help carry out the scheme of color and the aspect of comfort. It can be of the same material as the curtains and lambre-quin, or some fabric in keeping with them. A chess-table will be a desirable feature of the furnishings, if "my lord" loves the mimic fight, or even the more usual check-ers, and $12 will buy a good one. This table may serve suitably for the only one in the room, and a flat-top writing-desk may be added if there be space enough.   There will then be plenty of elbow-room for writing, and the top of the desk and its drawers will be sufficient to hold all the litter of papers and letters which a busy man may wish to leave untouched at home.   Such desks are not expensive, and may be found for from $10 to $20.   An old-fashioned secretary makes an acceptable furnishing when polished up, and can be utilized to advantage.

A smoker's set should be placed near at hand.   Such a set consists of a tray, match-safe, ash-receiver, and cigar-holder.   Fine ones are made of hammered brass, oxidized silver, and carved wood, while papier-maché, celluloid, and plain wood are used for cheaper grades.   Some are made of ebonized wood and mounted on a tripod or pedestal of the height of an ordinary table.   Prices of smoker's sets range from $15, the highest, to $1.25, the cheapest, while those on standards are about $2.   .

A lamp which will throw a good light

upon the book in hand and yet will shield the eyes is also needed. The student-lamp or the Rochester with its duplex burner is equally suitable, and $5 will supply a good one of either kind. Besides all these, a foot-rest, a slipper-case, an inkstand, a paper-rack, an afghan, and sofa pillows should be added to complete the furnishings to the comfort and liking of its occupant. They and other trifles give a wide range for choice of gifts when birthdays and Christmas draw near.

Is this too much to do for one individual in the household? Surely not, for your Benedict possesses all the virtues of American husbands and is generous to a fault to you, so spend freely of your time, taste, and trouble, and so much money as may be, and when dressed in your most becoming gown, you pour the social evening cup in his "den," his pride and delight in your efforts will not lack expression.

XIX.

HALLS AND WALLS.

MOST halls, both in city and country houses, are merely passage-ways, designed to give access to the different rooms and floors while using up as little space as possible. It is difficult to give such narrow halls any of the gracious touches which can be lavished so readily on the other rooms of a home. Still, it can be done to a small extent if the subject is considered thoughtfully.

A hall should be dignified in its aspect, but not forbidding and cheerless, and the first requisite to relieve it of its habitual gloom is to make it as light as possible. Where it can be done, a portion of the hall should be made into a vestibule. The double or single doors of this vestibule may be of solid wood, as heavy and massive as the style of the house permits; but these doors are better and handsomer when their upper panels are of glass. The inner door, opening directly into the hall, should always have full half its length of glass, either stained or ground, so that during the day light may pour into the hall, and make it less of a dark tunnel. The glass in the door, and also transoms over front doors where there is no vestibule, should be curtained, except in the instance of stained glass. The material of the curtain should be light in coloring and thin in texture, and not fulled on to rods or cords so thickly as to be equivalent to two layers of material. Madras, scrim, and dotted muslin are best adapted for this use.

Having let in as much light as may be, the next precaution is to increase its force by causing the large wall spaces to reflect the light, not absorb it. Whether paint, kalsomine, or paper be chosen for the wall, the colors should be light and warm. Indian yellow, Venetian red, buffs, light terracottas, or grays with warm lights in reds are the best colors for the hall. Paper is the most decorative wall finish, as its design re-

lieves the bareness of the long spaces; but
to be in keeping with the formal character of
a hall, the design should be geometrical, not
floral, bold and distinct, not fine and delicate. Patterns in Arabic or Greek figures
are particularly well suited to hall walls, for
the geometrical details of Saracenic ornament here find a natural place.

Wood carpet or hard-wood floors and
staircase are not pleasing in a hall, although
their aspect is rich and substantial. We
have not yet acquired the Japanese custom
of leaving our shoes outside the door, and
the hall gets the brunt of all the mud and
dust tracked into the house, which makes
such floors difficult to keep spotless. Of
the two the wood carpet is preferable, as its
cloth back deadens the sound of footsteps.
The constant travel through a hall with a
wood floor and up and down uncarpeted
stairs makes a great deal of clatter, which
pervades the whole house, and is wearisome
to the house-mother, who hears it oftener
than any one else, or to the invalid whose
nerves cannot endure racket unresentfully.
Body Brussels is the best carpet to buy, as

it will resist the wear and tear longest. Its design should also be geometrical and of a fine close pattern, rich in coloring, but not too dark. A black groundwork should be avoided, for it shows every trace of dust, as does a carpet whose coloring is largely red. A border on a hall carpet makes the room appear narrower, and for that reason the room looks better without one. Rugs, especially small ones, are apt to be stumbling-blocks, and should be sparingly used in a hall— one at the foot of the staircase and one at the door being generally sufficient. These should be chosen with taste and in keeping with the other fittings of the hall, but durability should be the first consideration. Choice rugs should be kept for rooms where they may be seen at better advantage.

In some modern halls the landing of the stairs is screened off by open wood-work, which can be made more decorative and effective by rich colored hangings behind it. But wherever hangings are used at the various door-ways, their colors should be those that will not absorb the light too much, although their texture should be heavy, to carry out the dignified character of the room. A Japanese bead and bamboo portière is an effective hanging for the door at the rear end of a hall, serving as a screen, and yet allowing the light to pass through it. Such portières cost about $4 a pair, and are more durable than would seem at first sight.

In a large or square hall the difficulty of treatment vanishes. Here can be had the tile or wood floor, or even a straw matting, with its surface well covered with a large rug, and thus hygiene and quiet would be propitiated. Besides the ordinary hall piece there could be chairs and a table in a wood matching the hall finish, a settle or bamboo lounge, and perhaps a corner fireplace. Suggestions for this kind of a hall are trite because any home-maker thus unhampered can make this room a charming place, a welcome to both the guest and the stranger.

The first furniture needed in a small hall is a hall piece, which should be as large as will be in proportion with the room. A small hall piece is unsatisfactory, because it always falls short of the demands upon it, and because the mirror which accompanies

it is "skimpy." This is the one place, outside a chamber, where a mirror is justified
by its usefulness. A place to see that one
is "all right" before appearing in public,
without an extra climb of stairs, will be ap-
preciated by every member of the family.
Hall pieces of moderate size can be found
in all woods for $25, and beyond that price
it is easy to satisfy one's taste under the
guidance of one's purse. Less expensive
substitutes, which when more prosperous
days come will find fields of usefulness in
other rooms, are a set of pegs, and, placed
underneath, a plain, good-sized table. Such
pegs with a fair-sized central mirror can be
bought for $5 to $10, and a table within the
same prices.

It is not pleasant for a stranger to stand
while waiting in a hall, and unless the hall
piece is large enough to include a seat, a
chair will add to the comfortable furnishings of the room. A small rush-bottomed
chair is more in harmony with ordinary
halls than any stiff-backed Gothic affair of
carved wood, which finds its natural place
in stately homes.

An umbrella-stand in tile is another needed outlay. Cheap ones cost as little as $2,
but higher - priced ones are more lasting.
Pictures get such poor light in a hall that
there is little inducement to hang them there;
but if one has an abundance, two or three of
bold design, engravings or photographs, will
rob the walls of their bareness.

A few words may be said about the basement hall of a city house. Treat it simi-
larly to the upper hall. Let the walls be
light and have an outer glass door. Except
a wood floor, nothing will resist the ungentle
tread of "the butcher, the baker, the candle-
stick-maker," whose daily visits are a necessity, like oil-cloth or linoleum, but get a
light-colored pattern resembling tiles. Put
a pretty colored shade over the gas-jet, or
let a gay lantern make decorative the gleams
of the kerosene flame, add a neat set of pegs
for the children's school coats and hats, and
you will have done much to relieve the ugli-
ness of this entry.

Whenever paper is to be used on the
walls of any room, not only the use of the
room, but its size, aspect, and its weak

points should be considered. A room with many windows in it looks better with paper of a darker tone than a room less abundantly lighted. A narrow room needs a color that will cause its walls to seem farther apart, while a large one will bear the reverse. A very high room will look better for a dado as well as a frieze, as this will decrease the apparent height. Few rooms need anything but a frieze, and in a low room this should be narrow, to increase the height. One rule always serves—that the main colors chosen should be darkest in the carpet, and gradually grow lighter in dado, wall space, and frieze, making the ceiling lightest of all. When trying to modify the apparent size of a room, it is useful to know that red is the only color which seems to produce no change, but preserves the actual size of the room. The different tints derived from it—pinks, terra-cottas, and the like—have partially this same property, and cause little apparent change in size. Yellow tints make walls seem nearer together, the less vivid or strong the tone the less the apparent approach. Blue tints make an effect of distance, which is shared in a lesser degree by greens and grays.

The different rooms of a home also demand different styles in designs, and in choosing patterns for the ordinary small homes small designs and light tints are best. American designs are also best, because foreign papers, especially the English, presuppose large rooms, and the designs are so large that they do not relieve or emphasize small walls sufficiently. For halls and dining-rooms, arabesque, geometrical designs are particularly suitable, and their richness in color should be chosen with regard to the outlook and lightness of the room. Bedrooms need something that is restful—that is to say, négligé—both in design and coloring. Pale soft tints and graceful intermingling patterns are in order. Bold figures, rigid geometrical monstrosities, wearisome horizontal or vertical lines, are a perfect nightmare to gaze on, and doubly so when ill. To a healthful person the idea that such walls torture an invalid seems mere nonsense, but even strong-minded persons have been known to weaken un-

der the baneful spell of rigid, haunting angles. The drawing-room and library need
richer designs and a touch of elegance to
harmonize with the other furnishings of the
rooms. Plain felt paper, cartridge, ingrain,
or granite, are equally suitable for such
rooms, and give a softer, less monotonous
tone than painted walls, as the fibre of the
paper shows through the color. For bath-
rooms, glazed tile-paper that can be cleaned
with soap and water is good, and can be
used equally well in kitchen, laundry, or
servant's quarters, though it is doubtful if
the variety the designs give the walls is of
enough value to supplant paint, which supplies so admirably the other qualifications
of wall finish for such rooms.

XX.

THE PARLOR.

THIS room is not absolutely essential to the House Comfortable, for it is the least used by the family, and in too many households is a closed and awful place, whose finery is chosen to equal or excel that of the caller and chance visitor. But in a busy home it is in no uncertain sense a comfort to the housewife to have one room always in order, ready for the reception of friend or acquaintance, who, with unconscious yet inevitable persistency, appears whenever matters are at their worst estate in the domestic kingdom. All housewives, even the wisest and most systematic, have suffered in such exigencies, and have been sustained by the comforting feeling that the parlor was presentable. At such times it becomes a harbor of refuge, and at all times the pretty room gives a sense of social security and satisfaction which even the most convenient kitchen or hygienic bedrooms cannot compass.

Much has been said by writers, domestic and æsthetic, on the drawing-room, and consequently greater prominence has been commonly given the room than to others in the home. But although the room is important to us in social ways, and with its beautiful adornings is a fitting crown and ornament to the whole home, yet we must remember that "the ideal home is largely the handiwork of the contented mind." The home should, first of all, be sufficient for the domestic needs and comforts, and after that for the requirements of society. In furnishing our parlor we should endeavor to attain such rare mental poise that our minds should be contented to choose those fittings in harmony with not only the exchequer, but with the other domestic surroundings. If we attempt to furnish up to our neighbor's standard, we shall produce nothing but a room at odds with all our other possessions; a whole room full of discontent if we have the inner

vision quick to discern it. With a contented mind, which is potent to clear the judg-
ment and rectify the taste, let the housewife
begin furnishing her parlor, or her drawing-
room, if her scale of living is large enough to
justify the more fashionable word.

No other room of a home needs so much
the benefit of growth in matters of taste as
this, and for that reason it is not a calamity
if the furnishings must be gradually bought,
and if vacant spaces must wait for further
adornment. One's own experience can readily call to mind the awful and tasteless splen-
dors of parlors whose ill-fortune it was to be
furnished all at once. The parlor is not
only the pride of the house, but the measure
of the family culture, and it should be the
abode of refinement. To achieve this in a
small home, one should buy cautiously and
slowly, and always such articles as are thoroughly substantial—not flashy—letting the
designs be as graceful and decorative as
possible. The aim should be to have all
the large furnishings express quietness,
leaving the dashes of brightness and oddity
to be supplied by small articles. These

13

odd pieces are too often the mere fads of
the hour. When their reign is passed, they
annoy, and we wish to rid ourselves of them,
which can easily be done when they are
small and comparatively inexpensive.

A handsome carpet is by all odds the
cheapest floor-covering, and in most homes
will be the best adapted to the other furnishings. Rugs are more beautiful if the gem-
like ones of Oriental weaving and design
can be chosen; but to get those of sufficient
size to do away with a carpet entirely requires a large outlay. The parlor carpet
does not become so dusty, and its use there
is not so objectionable, as in dining or sitting-room. The depth of color in the chosen
carpet and rugs must depend on the color
of the wood-work and walls. If you wish
to have your drawing-room in white and
gold, it is well to know at the outset that
this will be expensive. Five to nine coats
of paint are needed, for less than five will
not give the lustrous ivory finish which is
the beauty of this style of decoration. With
wood-work in dark stains or natural colors
of the wood, a darker carpet can be used

than with the white and gold treatment, although it is safe to say that no ordinary parlor will be tasteful and cheerful with darker carpets than dealers class as "medium dark."

If a paper is chosen for the walls, let the design be free and rich, but beware of high colors or over-display of metallic effects. Cartridge-papers in plain tints are excellent and tasteful, and form a beautiful background for etchings, engravings, and other ornaments.   It is true that such paper needs an abundance of pictures, else the plain background is monotonous, but a blank wall space is bearable when one knows that the next new picture will harmonize all, and be in turn beautified by the delicate background.

The most popular wood for furniture is the sixteenth-century oak; that is to say, modern oak stained in imitation of age.   But the wise buyer will not invest in this wood exclusively, for she will recall the days when mahogany was the fashionable wood, of its displacement by black walnut, and the latter in turn by the now popular oak.   Neither

will she buy a "parlor suit." These, with
their many pieces, are the relic of a more
primitive taste. Now the conventional set
is three pieces—a sofa and two chairs. It
is well to have so many pieces of the same
kind to serve as a nucleus of furnishing, lest
having every chair unlike produce a "helter-
skelter " effect. Broad, low-seated chairs
and sofas are the prevailing and comfortable
style, but there are people with eccentric
spines and limbs who are only comfortable
in high, straight chairs, and for their sakes
let one chair in the parlor be of this description. One or two chairs of bamboo
or rattan, which can be easily and quickly
moved to any side of the room, are also
quite indispensable, as upholstered furniture
is heavy and clumsy.

Raw silk, which is largely made of hemp
and wool, is the favorite covering for furniture, but velvet is the most durable. Besides
these are the plushes, spun silk, furniture
damask, or brocade, which is comparatively
light in weight, the heavier brocatelle, and
countless varieties of velours, reps, and the
like. These nearly all come 48 or 52 inches

wide, and the following prices are inserted
as a slight guide to those who wish to re-
cover old furniture: raw silk, 45 cents to
$1.25; spun silk, $1.25 to $4; velours,
$2.50; velvet, $4. Letter " S " double chairs
are popular, and cost from $30 to $70, while
single chairs of handsome pattern are $15
and upwards. The conventional set costs
about $30, while pretty tables of oak or
cherry cost $6 to $20, rosewood being more
costly. Pedestals for statuettes or large
vases cost $5 to $10 in all the ordinary
woods.

Among the more recent means of ornament to a parlor are transoms of open-work
in wood, bamboo, or brass to be placed in
the tops of window-casings and door-frames,
the curtains and portières being hung beneath them. These lessen the height of
long windows and doors, and are only suitable in rooms which are at least ten feet
high. These transoms come in sections,
and are sold by the foot, the price varying
with the design and material.

Cabinets, with dainty jug, fragile vase, or
gleaming silver trifle shining through their

crystal-clear doors, transform into a picture vacant spaces. Hanging cabinets of oak or cherry cost $20 to $45, while those of ebonized wood cost $20 to $75. Large cabinets standing on the floor cost $30 at least, while for an easel for your favorite picture and corner you may pay $1 for one of bamboo, or $30 for one of ebonized wood.

In choosing the ornaments of a parlor, the home-maker should again make haste slowly. Cheap ornaments may please for a time, but it is better to select the vase, ceramic, brass or bronze bits for mantel or table, with cautious discrimination, and not to fritter away money on a multitude of trifles which have slight value. It is incongruous to put a pair of dollar vases either side a really fine clock; and so doing at least indicates the buyer's lack of patience, if not her ignorance and tastelessness. Better the traditional aching void till " the ship comes in " than such a glaring misfit. Besides avoiding the danger of cheap and superfluous ornaments, let there be a restraining hand in the use of draperies, ribbons, sachet-bags, and banners — adornments that, applied within bounds, give artistic and dainty touches to a pleasant room ; but used freely, they make a silly, littered, uncultivated room, wholly out of touch with the House Comfortable.

XXI.

LIBRARY AND MUSIC-ROOM.

NOT every one possesses a library, but where there is a large and steady accumulation of books it is best to set apart a room for them. Small bookcases in sitting-room and chamber are useful to hold the favorite and oft-consulted volumes, but for the mass of books a library with ample shelves is the natural place. Large piles of books in every available spot on table, mantel, and floor in the common rooms of a home involve a vast amount of needless labor in the dusting and cleaning. Besides the extra work of handling the books over and over, it is far easier to find a book when it has a home of its own on some accustomed shelf than to hunt over irregular and shifting piles. These practical claims for a permanent home for these silent companions of the varied hours

and moods of life are small beside the affec-
tionate care which a true lover of books
feels for his treasures. "Reading maketh a
full man," wrote Bacon, and no matter how
limited the resources or how small the home,
when this desire to be filled enters into home
life books will be there, and upon the home-
maker devolves the problem of finding abid-
ing-places for them.

A small room on either the ground or
chamber floor is well adapted for a library
where the accumulations are not liable to
become very great. It is not necessary
that the outlook of such a room be pleasant
or sunny, for whether far away in the realms
of fancy or living over the lives of real or
imaginary heroes, no book-lover cares whether the view be charming or the day serene.
All that he asks is a comfortable chair,
plenty of light, and undisturbed peace. It
is these latter needs that give the home
mother the key to the furnishings of such a
room. Having selected the room, she must
study to obtain serenity and repose in its
fittings.

The walls may be rather soberer in coloring than other rooms, but by no means should the color be so sombre as to make the room sepulchral in feeling. The design, in case wall-paper is used, should be rich; but loud, flaring, naturalistic patterns are especially to be avoided. When one is doubtful what to choose, the plain felt papers in brown, chocolate, old green, olive, blue-gray, or terra-cotta make excellent and tasteful selections. The wood floor in some of its various forms is the comfortable floor treatment. Constant sweeping and dust-making from a carpet is not conducive to intellectual repose or any improvement to the books upon the shelves. Next best to the wood floor is a plain matting in a dark tint, matching or harmonizing with the wall tint. Then rugs may be added, as many as you please. However much the windows of other rooms may be draped, here one should restrain the hand. In this room the æsthetic sense is to be but a humble background for the play of the intellectual faculties, and nothing must interfere with the easeful labor of the eyes in lighting up the inner vision. Simple, harmonious shades are the first needs of library windows. After that rich-tinted, easy-moving curtains of chenille or other heavy fabrics carry out the decorative scheme of the room if there are many windows. If but one, let the hangings be of some thin goods which will not cut off any light.

Low bookcases not more than five feet in height are to be chosen whenever one can furnish from the beginning. In a permanent home, shelving fitted into the walls is the best arrangement, especially where books increase continually. These shelves can be of natural woods like the finish of the room, or stained woods. The cost, of course, will vary with the size of the room and the kind of wood, but generally such shelves cost less than a case from the cabinet-maker's which will hold a hundred volumes. A contrivance for book-shelves which can be removed whenever the Lares and Penates go into a moving van is a series of boxes, neatly and strongly made, coverless, and of the same length. The width of the boxes should vary according to the different sizes of your books, while the depth should be uniform.

Place the boxes in rows, on their sides, one above another, and, presto! you have movable shelves that will serve as packing-boxes when your books must travel. Small, low bookcases, costing from $10 to $25, are the manageable size if one prefers to furnish in a more showy and handsomer style. But whatever the choice, be sure to have empty shelves enough. Bookcases should always have plenty of room for book growth. Cases with glass doors are more costly, and except for rare treasures, the doors are a useless separation of the printed pages from the reader. Curtains of any drapery fabric that seems suitable are a sufficient protection from dust, and less forbidding than glass doors, besides offering another opportunity for the deft fancy and nimble fingers of the decorator of the household.

Over the bookcases there will be ample space to hang the family portraits. Here they will look down on their kith and kin, and with approving glances seem to sympathize with or stimulate the thoughts of the living reader, while chilled by no careless looks from indifferent strangers. Bronzes, plaster casts, large porcelain ornaments, also find a suitable resting-place on the bookcase top, and add an interesting aspect to the room.

Any comfortable chairs can be chosen, although leather is the suitable material for the upholstering. Leather-covered lounges in green, brown, or dark red cost $28, while easy-chairs cost about $20. A revolving chair for a desk, in bent-wood, costs $4 to $6, but with leather upholstering, $7 to $20. A library usually has a desk, for the quietness of the room is favorable to writing. Ordinary desks, which close by raising the writing-table, cost from $20 to $40; a flat-top desk like a large table, and with capacious drawers, costs about $20; while the roller-top desk costs from $25 to $80, the latter being of office size, and with every convenience for business. If your library has no desk, or but a small one, add to it a generous table, costing from $16 to $40, with a fine lamp or drop-light upon it.

In these suggestions it has been intended to give an outline of the suitable fittings of a library, leaving it for the reader to fill in the details as means, materials, and taste may prompt her. Many country and town homes have a large upper hall, which could be appropriately fitted up for a library without encroaching on other household arrangements, while in small families its general fittings can be discreetly combined with those of "the family hearth-stone," and be satisfactory to all interested.

Few families require both a music-room and a library, and in a home where the musical tastes predominate the unused room is most acceptable when made into a music-room. In such a room there should be good light, and nothing to muffle and obstruct the sounds. The floor should be uncarpeted, and the furniture entirely without upholstery. Draperies should be wholly tabooed, for the genuine musician's soul is rapt, listening to divine harmonies, and all outward, discordant things, however decorative, are abhorred. A light, cheerful tint should relieve the walls, one that looks prettily by artificial light being preferred, as the room will be the most sought at this time.

Bamboo or rattan furniture is among the prettiest for this room. Small chairs in rattan cost from $4 to $10, and the arm-chairs cost $5 to $12. A rattan sofa costs from $10 to $20, while bamboo chairs in silver, gilt, or copper are $5 to $8; and stained wood, rush-seated, cost $4. Much cheaper rush or cane bottomed chairs are equally comfortable, and can be substituted for the more showy rattan.

Old-time music-racks were seldom capacious, and were unhandy. The modern ones are really cabinets. They stand about five feet high, and their shelves and drawers are especially convenient for sheet-music, protecting it from being tumbled and torn. Such music-racks, plainly made, cost $10, while elaborate ones cost as high as $50. Tall lamps to stand on the floor beside the piano are made with standards in nickel, brass, and wrought-iron. The cheaper ones cost $10, and others vary in price from that amount up to $100. A lamp with a reflector behind it is more modest, but equally efficient. It should be fastened to the wall so that its light will be focussed on the music-rack of the piano. Pretty lamps of this sort costs $3.

Pictures of the masters of harmony, scenes from the various operas, and busts of composers or ideal heads of musical heroes form fitting ornaments to such a room. But when the piano is open, the violin in tune, and flute and banjo mingle their notes in the family orchestra, then is the music-room best fulfilling its destiny and adding to the comfort and pleasure of both players and listeners.

XXII.

TREASURE-CHAMBERS.

THE careful housewife knows that her attic or storeroom and her closets are veritable treasure-chambers, for in them she stores the serviceable garments, the useful box, the handy table and chairs, waiting for the opportune moment when each shall be returned to active service. To the housewife at least the convenient and orderly arrangement of her treasure-chambers is a matter of genuine importance. Upon her alone falls the care of these retreats, and in the searches for missed or wished-for articles she is usually chief if not sole actor.

The average height of women is five feet two inches; but rarely does one find a house, in city or country, in which any attention has been paid to this fact in arranging the closets. The hooks are placed fully six feet from the

14

floor, and lucky for the housewife if it is not more, and above them is placed a shelf which is practically almost useless. No woman cares to mount a chair or table every time she wishes to get her bonnet, her shawl, or her bottle of blacking, and the result is a series of boxes standing on the floor, which, though handy, have to be moved with every sweeping. The ideal closet has the cleat on which the hooks are screwed on the side and ends of the closet only four and a half or five feet from the floor, with the shelf only two or three inches above it. Besides this series of hooks a double or single row of double hooks, shaped like an inverted T, are screwed into the under-side of the shelf, thereby doubling the capacity of the closet. Another plan, even better, is in addition to the usual row of hooks on the wall to have a movable cleat or rod across the middle of the closet lengthwise, and fastened to it a number of movable hooks made of galvanized wire. On these wire hooks clothing can be hung closely and pushed along to make more room, in the same manner as coats and dresses are hung in ready-made clothing-shops. Clothing of all kinds keeps in much better shape when hung on yokes. An economical means of supplying an unlimited number of these is to take pieces of barrel hoops, twelve inches long, and wind each with old cambric or muslin. Woollen cloth is unsuitable for this use, as it offers too convenient lodgings for moths. Then make a loop at the centre of each yoke with stout cord, wire, or cloth, and the yokes are ready for use.

The floors of closets, with their wide cracks, are troublesome in collecting lint and dust, besides making safe homes for moths and beetles. In a permanent home these cracks should always be filled, and in a rented house the time it takes to do this is usually less than the vexation which the lodgement of household pests causes. Putty, plaster of Paris, or even newspaper shredded finely and made into a paste with hot water and a little glue, will fill the cracks nicely. Plaster of Paris is the easiest to use and most satisfactory in results, but, as it hardens very rapidly, only a little should be prepared at a time. The powder is mixed with enough cold water to make the paste of the right consistency to spread, and then filled in with a common steel knife. After the cracks are filled and hard, two coats of paint should be given the floor to make it look neat and smooth.

Closets devoted to shelves are apt to have the shelves too far apart, causing the first shelf to be the only one of much value. The average carpenter puts the shelves in every closet impartially twenty inches apart. In linen closets, or closets devoted to storing blankets and other bedding, such generous spaces are well suited; but in the ordinary cupboard twelve or fifteen inches between shelves is ample space, and allows two or three shelves to be convenient for general use.

The protection of clothing from insect enemies when stored away is an unending bother. The wary beetle and the elusive moth-miller scoff at camphor, enjoy tarine balls, crawl calmly over tarred paper, wiggle through cracks of the cedar closet, and persistently edge their way impartially into cedar or pine box. The only safety is to put clean (either sponged, washed, or steamed), well-beaten, well-sunned garments first into muslin, either old or coarse, and then to wrap closely in newspaper. Insects have no appetite for either cotton or printer's ink. This double precaution, however, makes it impossible to tell one garment from another in its mummy-like wrappings, so it follows that every parcel must be labelled. Then it is difficult to remember which closet has this or that parcel. A large sheet of paper tacked on the inside of each closet door or lid of chest or trunk makes it easy to write down each bundle as it is put away, and will show at any time the contents of each receptacle. The shoe and bundle bags are great aids to orderly closets, and in them there should be a place for wrapping-paper and pieces or a ball of twine.

The joys of playing in an attic in stormy weather are among the best-remembered pleasures of childhood. Such a treasure-trove it was to eager childish hearts! Such lively games, and such noisy shouts as its walls echoed! And, best of all, what book so interesting as that one we read in the attic, wrapped in a comforter, while on the roof came the cold April rain, rattling the loose shingles as it fell? But what did our mothers think when they beheld our clothing, torn on unwary nails, covered with cobwebs, and begrimed with ancient dusts? To a modern child the attic is equally attractive, although the house-keeper of to-day generally has " advanced ideas " of cleanliness and order.

When one builds a house, one should have the attic lathed and plastered like the rest of the house, and have a tight floor laid. The loose floor-boards, exposed beams, and unfinished walls give too much freedom to rats and mice, and make it hard to give the attic its two sweepings and moppings yearly.

The attic is too frequently the catch-all for broken things. Legless chairs, hoopless pails, disabled lamps, old shoes, and trunks with broken hinges here find a common meeting - ground. But if anything seems worth keeping, have it mended, and do not carry to the attic things that can never again be useful. As far as possible, put things that are alike together — trunks in one place, boxes in another, furniture in this corner, and the long lengths of winter stove-pipes with their elbows in that side. Let the key of each trunk be tied to it, and in each one put the leather strap or canvas cover that goes with it. If chairs are put away that have woollen upholstery, cover them tightly with old muslin. Here in a box put all the tools used for domestic carpentry, excepting perhaps a hammer and a box of tacks and nails, whose frequent use will give them a home in a kitchen drawer. Empty spice-boxes, labelled, make good receptacles for nails, screws, bolts, and buttons, while pasteboard boxes will hold the extra casters, the rolls of wire, bits of sandpaper—the whole to be kept in one wooden box, ready to be carried to any room where repairs are needed.

A storeroom is like a miniature attic, easier of access, but not so capacious. Here are shelves to store clothing and bedding, and crowded and wedged under them and along the floor are superfluous furniture and trunks. Little childish romance hangs about this room, for it is too small and dark for play.   But what an appetizing place is the storeroom which holds the fruits, herbs, and groceries for home consumption!   Such a storeroom is an actual necessity in a family of any size.   Here should be stored all food supplies not wanted for immediate use. Economical buying of groceries in large quantities needs to be allied to the thrifty use of them to be effectual, and how easy to be lavish when large amounts are constantly at hand in the kitchen!   This storeroom should be light, and well supplied with shelving, and one cupboard or curtained corner for those preserves which do not bear the light.   The dry groceries kept in a storeroom should be put in tight cans of tin, glass, or earthen-ware; herbs in tight bags; and flour in close sacks or barrels. Each article should be labelled, and great care taken that nothing is spilled in dealing out the supplies.   Then, with clean shelves, good things in orderly rows, the housewife can calmly turn the key to go to other duties.

XXIII.

A CATCH-ALL CHAPTER.

THERE are many things which are important to the comfort of a house, yet which
do not require a whole chapter to themselves. There is mother's corner, for instance. It is seldom a whole room, often
nothing but a low chair, with a small table
beside it for her work-basket, in a sunny
window of sitting-room, dining-room, or bedroom. Sometimes, indeed, it has a table
with mother's favorite books, or perhaps
with her paints, palette, and easel; but
wherever it may be it is almost certain-
ly the centre of the family life, the spot
to which perplexities and trials are taken,
and where wisdom and courage are found
to inspire all the members of the family.
But how often is it as well furnished as it
might be? How often is the chair the

easiest and are the little adornings the prettiest in the house? Surely every member of the family will feel that these should be the best; but when mother has been left to furnish her own corner as well as the rest of the house, the easiest chair has too often been saved for father, and the handsomest things have gone into the parlor; so that if mother's corner is a cosey place, it is because mother's presence irradiates second - best things. Here is a promising field of domestic reform open to growing daughters and sons, and worthy the attention of the head of the house if these lines should fall under his eye, to remind him of an omission which is due to want of thought rather than to lack of will.

The hospitable spirit of a family finds fitting expression in a guest-chamber, wherever it is possible to set aside a room for such a purpose. It is a mistake, however, to take the largest and pleasantest chamber for guests, causing the daughter and son to use gloomy small rooms the year around, while the better room is without an occupant weeks at a time. For the chance and tran-

sitory visitor the small room cosily furnished
is just as inviting, and in no sense limits
your welcome of him. But in a guest's room
one should aim to have simplicity of furnishings. Plentiful and delicate draperies
embarrass a careful visitor; he fears lest
he soil them, tear them, or worries over all
sorts of imagined mishaps. The careful
and careless visitor alike are liable to tip
over the ink-bottle, the cologne, or the bottle of medicine, and then all the laborious
embroidery, the fresh ribbons, and delicate
laces of the toilet set are ruined. Whatever
the feelings of our guest about the mishap,
our own are apt to be anything but serene.
It is better, then, to have these graceful ac-
cessaries of the toilet of a simple nature,
easily laundered, and of comparatively inexpensive material. A davenport is a particularly gratifying piece of furniture to a
guest, and when the scale of living is sufficiently ample and the size of the room
admits of it, it should be always present.
Pretty little davenports, in oak or cherry,
can be bought for $10 to $15 ; while a writing-table with a drawer may be easily fitted

up to answer the purpose. An undraped large lamp, a few books and recent magazines, and an easy-chair and footstool are trifles which the guest—stranger or friend —will thoroughly appreciate.

The servant's room should have its share of considerate attention, for a home cannot be the House Comfortable when the needs of any of its inmates are overlooked. In spite of much written and spoken to the contrary, it is the exceptional servant who will bestow on her room the care it should receive without constant watching and urging from her employer. So it is best to reduce the care to the smallest amount compatible with comfort, and to select a small room. An iron bedstead is the cleanest for such a room, and a single bed costs from $8 to $12, including the springs, while a plain hard-wood bedstead and springs can be bought for $5. Besides warm colored blankets or comforters and white coverlet, there should be a good mattress, for who better deserves a comfortable resting-place than the servant who is on her feet from early morning till late at night?

A stained floor, with a piece of carpet or a rug before the bed, is preferable, but is not always to be commanded. Next to this comes oil-cloth or an ingrain carpet, straw matting being not sufficiently durable. A plain bureau or chest of drawers costs $4 or $5, while a mirror, wash-sink, and plain earthen toilet set cost $6. Painted iron standards, with wash-basin, pitcher, and slop-jar, are sold for $4, and are admirable in small rooms. If there is no closet, one can be improvised by curtaining off one corner of the room, and supplying it with rows of hooks. Order cannot be expected where there are no facilities to encourage it, and too often the servant's room is like this odd definition of chaos: "A little of everything, and no place to put it in." Simple white curtains and coverings for the bureau give the room a homelike, womanly touch, but whatever they are let them be of wash materials. A tidy servant likes snow-white cloths about her, and an untidy one will not try to keep colored drapings clean. A rocking-chair should be added when space will allow it, and if one or two pictures or a banner should be fastened on the bare wall, it will gratify a good servant. A poor servant will not be more incompetent from the influences of a room which shows that her employer appreciates the fact that she is a fellow-being and a woman too.

The daughter's room is the place where daintiness should reign. As soon as a little girl is old enough to be interested in her room, and to be willing to give it the personal care requisite, she should not only be allowed, but be encouraged to express her personal tastes, to choose the general coloring, and to collect in her room all those pretty and instructive belongings that interest her. What the details may be will vary with the daughter, but the general outline will be the same. If parental means are small, the special pieces of furniture, such as bookcases or shelves, writing-desk, the little "consideration" chair, where she will sit to think over matters in general and particular, can be gifts on birthdays or bought out of the girl's own allowance, and fitted up with the ingenious contrivings of her nimble wits, aided by her deft fingers. If

the daughter inclines to a multitude of drapings, the mother must restrain her own sanitary impulses.   She must explain the necessity of keeping the draperies free from dust,
and insist upon its being done.   But she
must remember that at no other time will
the daughter have a better chance to gratify
innocent delights, and not repress the young
girl's taste too closely.

The son, too, has his ideals of a pleasant
room, and, besides the justice of giving him
his rights in his own domain, many lessons
of order, taste, and comfort are unconscious-
ly enforced, and sometimes special tastes
and gifts receive such an impetus as to be
valuable factors in deciding the boy's business calling.   A boy does not care for frip-
peries.   He does appreciate a tidy room
which would seem prim and bare to his
sister's taste.   Better than window draperies to him are shelves for his minerals or
birds' eggs.   A big drawer in a bureau or
table, nicely lined, in which to fasten his
collection of butterflies and bugs, is a real
bonanza to him, while a wall-cabinet, however cheaply gotten up, but with glass doors

to shield his treasures, is as great a delight to him as a pretty work-basket is to his sister. To be sure, his spasms of making collections may be intermittent and short-lived, but they are genuine for the time, and to give him place for his treasures is wise and just.

If the son has a mechanical taste, let him have a tool-box, a turning-lathe, or wood-carving implements. A square of oil-cloth will catch all the shavings and litter, and perhaps he will sweep them up himself. If he does not, it is "clean dirt," and easily removed. Have a place for his books, a shelf or hooks for his skates and his catcher cage or gloves, if he affects base-ball. If it is possible to rig a horizontal bar, so much the better; and, at all events, let a pair of dumb-bells and Indian clubs have a special corner. Mount the blue prints of his photographic friends' or his own production, and frame the picture of his favorite crew or ball nine, explorer, or mountain-climber, even if the pictures are only coarse wood-cuts and the frames stained pine. The room will not, perhaps, suit you, O mother, but it will delight your son, and he will never forget its pleasantness, though the roof be low. Much less will he forget the loving thoughtfulness that wrought such a pleasant nest.

15

XXIV.

OUT IN THE BACK YARD.

THE back yard is apt to be the dumping-
ground for all that is useless in the house,
and the mere mention of the name calls up
anything but an agreeable mental picture.
But the back yard is the house-keeper's
friend, and if rightly managed can be as
attractive in its way as any part of the domestic realm. The front yard or lawn be-
longs, it is cynically said, to one's neighbors,
while the back yard is ours alone. Here,
under the influence of the sun and air, is
completed the purifying of household belongings, and here are growing the flowers
or fruit, the herb or vegetable, that fill the
eye, please the palate, and nourish the body.

The first requisite of a back yard truly
allied to the comfort of a household is that
it shall be well drained. To have it damp

from standing water, littered and soggy from household refuse, makes it impossible to be anything but an eyesore, while, in addition, it is a constant danger to the health of all within its influence. In large cities and towns, where there is a system of sewerage, the proper drainage can easily be secured. In small villages and the country the difficulty is great, but the need even greater. People in these fortunate places have plenty of room, and for that reason have not been compelled to have their premises sanitarily clean as the dwellers in crowded cities are obliged to do. But the water from sinks and drains must be carried off as far as possible from the dwelling, and then let nature's disinfectants, the sun, air, and earth, do their beneficent work. Every solid substance should be carefully excluded from these drains and destroyed by burning. This is the only sanitary disposition of garbage, and each family should burn its own daily. Where domestic animals are kept much can be fed to them, and on farms the remainder thrown on the compost heap.

Besides the unsightly refuse, the back

yard is too often scarred with piles of broken glass, dishes, and discarded tin cans. All such things will accumulate in every house, and the best method of disposing of them is to have a barrel or cask tidily set aside to throw them in; and when the receptacle is full the junkman or the village dump is ready to receive them. Another barrel should also be ready for all the odds and ends — the torn wrapping paper, the superfluous and dirty papers, the worn-out bits of carpet, and all kindred things that are too large to burn up in the kitchen fire. Then when the garden rubbish is burned each spring these will help kindle the flames. Coal-ashes are another troublesome commodity. As they cannot be cured, they must be endured, but their heap should be as compact and retired as may be, and thoroughly cleared away every spring. These ashes, well packed down, make passable walks between garden beds, and are often used to fill up hollows and holes, with a liberal coating of earth over them.

When the back yard has been well drained and freed from rubbish, a large part of it should be sown to grass. A nice bit of grass kept as neatly as a lawn is the housewife's pride. Here she spreads her household linen, and bleaches it until "snowy white" is no mere phrase. Here are removed all stains, and all traces of ill odors are replaced with the freshness of evening breeze and morning dews. Here the housewife stretches the lines, and hangs her bedding and clothes, that her home may be free from that stuffiness of atmosphere which surely indicates a careless home-maker.

When there is space enough there should be a garden in the back yard, where early vegetables can be grown in such kind and number as the family tastes may decide. Sage, thyme, balm, and sweet-marjoram are a great help to the housewife, making savory many otherwise plain dishes, and are especially fitting to grow in a back yard. Small fruits, too, will fill many a vacant spot, and in their season add to the family comfort, while their care and growth will be a constant pleasure to the family gardener.

Fences to divide the front and back yards, or to shut off the portion made into a garden, are seldom successful or ornamental. They get loose and rattling in post and picket, and hingeless and sagging in regard to gates. A hedge of barberry, arbor-vitæ, or cedar or osage orange is far better, although it takes a few years to get these to grow properly, and they may need a slight fence to protect them during the first years of growth. A screen between the vegetable garden and the front lawn is desirable. A trellis of grape-vines supplies this admirably, for no vine is handsomer or affords a more complete screen than the grape, while by selecting the variety suitable to the climate one may have much delicious fruit. But when something of more rapid growth is wanted, flowering climbers are best, and with morning-glory or flowering beans, cypress-vine or honeysuckle, climbing rose or woodbine, besides countless others, to choose from, there is room for all varieties of taste. A hedge of sweet-pease makes another beautiful screen when sown liberally and deeply, and supported by brush, like vegetable pease.

The city home-maker can, if she chooses,

easily make her back yard a thing of beauty.
The ashman, the garbage - man, and the
junkman are her aids in disposing of all
refuse.   At least she can have a neat grass-
plot to remind her of green fields far away.
Where the city home is not closed during
the summer months it is a great addition
to the family pleasure to have as much of
a garden as possible.   The centre space
should be left in grass; but with long narrow beds running between the pen - like
fence and the stone walk on both sides of
the yard, and the bed running the whole
width of the lot at the farther end, there is
room to do wonders.   Three or four small
fruit trees, such as pear, peach, or cherry,
can be set out at intervals, while a grape-
vine will make a handsome background
of the rear fence.   Small climbers should
be planted along the side fences to shut
out unsightliness.   Roses, chrysanthemums,
and perennials of many sorts are most satisfactory, giving little trouble, while the cheerful geranium, the bell-like fuchsia, the bright-
eyed pansy, and thrifty verbena will furnish
quantities of blossoms throughout the sea-

son. A couple of tomato-plants, or a half-dozen hills of dwarf string-beans can be smuggled in, and one can have the supreme pleasure of eating of the fruits of one's own labor.

There is one vegetable seldom found in fresh condition in city markets, and that is asparagus. This does not require large space, and, once started, will almost care for itself for years. Here, then, is a new field of labor for the domestic gardener who is, above all things, practical.

Where a city house is deserted in the hot season, seedlings and delicate plants should not be attempted, as they need daily care. Hardy perennials, shrubs, and climbing vines should then be chosen, which can be left to their own devices through the summer, with the addition of a bed of bulbs, tulip, crocus, and hyacinth, that bloom long before the yearly exodus.

THE END.